Grandpa ..
Chatterji

and

GRANDPA'S
INDIAN SUMMER

JAMILA GAVIN

Grandpa **Chatterji**

and

GRANDPA'S INDIAN SUMMER

Illustrated by Mei-Yim Low

mammoth

First published in Great Britain as two separate volumes:

Grandpa Chatterji
First published in Great Britain 1993
by Methuen Children's Books Ltd
Published 1994 by Mammoth
Text copyright © 1993 Jamila Gavin
Illustrations copyright © 1993 Mei-Yim Low

Grandpa's Indian Summer
First published in Great Britain 1995
by Methuen Children's Books Ltd
Published 1996 by Mammoth
Text copyright © 1995 Jamila Gavin
Illustrations copyright © 1995 Mei-Yim Low
Cover illustration © 1995 Duncan Smith

This omnibus edition first published 1999 by Mammoth
an imprint of Egmont Children's Books Limited
239 Kensington High Street, London W8 6SA

The moral rights of the author and the illustrator have been asserted.

ISBN 0 7497 4091 4

A CIP catalogue record for this title
is available from the British Library

Printed in Great Britain
by Cox & Wyman Ltd, Reading, Berkshire

Contents

1

'What are you doing, Grandpa?'

Neetu and her little brother Sanjay have two grandpas – Mum's dad and Dad's dad.

Mum's dad lives in India and they have never ever seen him. But Dad's dad lives in Leicester and they see him quite often.

Although they love and respect Dad's dad, as head of the family, Neetu and Sanjay are a little afraid of him. Whenever he comes to visit, they all have to be on their toes.

If Neetu wears jeans, Grandpa Leicester frowns at her and snorts, 'I don't like my granddaughter wearing jeans,' so she has to go and put on a dress. If Sanjay, who is a terrible chatterbox, sometimes interrupts, Grandfather glares at him sternly and says, 'I don't like little boys who interrupt,' and Sanjay has to bite his lip and try so hard not to speak.

When their mother got a job and went out to work, Grandfather was very disapproving. 'I don't like my daughter-in-law going out to work.' Mum just smiled politely, and went anyway, and Dad took his father aside to try to explain how with Mum going to work, they could afford a new car.

Perhaps the worst time is when Dad's dad comes to stay and they can't eat their favourite pizza and chips. Instead, they have to eat vegetable curry, runny spinach with eggs, and horrible stuff like that.

One day, Mum said excitedly, 'Children! Your grandpa is coming to stay! Isn't that wonderful!' But they didn't think it was wonderful at all. Neetu just groaned and said, 'Oh no! I'll have to wear nothing but dresses,' and Sanjay moaned, 'Oh no! We'll have to eat curried eggs.'

It was Dad who beamed at them and said, 'It's not my dad from Leicester who's coming to visit us, it's your Mum's dad from Calcutta. You've never met him! You can call him "Grandpa Chatterji".'

Neetu and Sanjay looked at each other doubtfully. How could they know whether a grandad from Calcutta was any different from a

grandad from Leicester, even if he was called Grandpa Chatterji? They would just have to wait and see.

All that week Mum went round with a smile on her face, and even Dad seemed quite relaxed. Mum got the spare room ready, just as she always did for Dad's dad. But instead of worriedly scrubbing and cleaning and polishing and checking that there was not one speck of dust to be seen anywhere in the house, she actually hummed and sang and seemed to enjoy making everything look nice.

On the day of his arrival, Mum and Dad got up very early and drove off to the airport to meet Grandpa Chatterji. Neetu and Sanjay didn't go because there wouldn't be room in the car on the way back. Old Mrs Bennet from next door came in to look after them.

They waited and waited. Sanjay looked out of one window and Neetu looked out of the other. What would he be like? Would he wear a smart suit and shiny black shoes like Dad's dad? Would he smoke cigars and sit in the best easy chair and talk business with Dad in a big boomy voice? Would he have the best bed? Would he be served first at table? Would he always insist on using the bathroom first in the morning, even though he took the longest and made them late for school? And would he be critical and strict and insist on total obedience at all times?

They waited and waited. Suddenly, Sanjay shouted, 'They're here!' The little red Mini had pulled up outside the house.

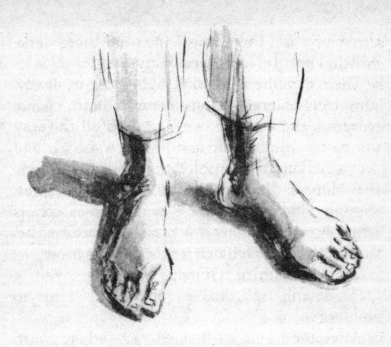

'Oh dear,' cried Neetu, suddenly going all shy, 'I'm going to hide.'

They both hid behind the sofa. They heard the front door open. They heard Mum come in and say gently, 'Welcome to our home!' They heard Dad say, 'I'll take your luggage up to your room,' and they heard a thin, quiet, soft voice say, 'And where are my little grandchildren?'

Then there was silence. Crouched behind the sofa, Neetu and Sanjay hardly breathed. Then suddenly, although they didn't hear Grandpa Chatterji come into the room, they knew he was there because they saw a pair of bare, dark-brown, knobbly, long-toed, bony feet.

The feet came and stood right close by them. The feet emerged from beneath thin, white trousers, and as their eyes travelled all the way up, past a white tunic and brown waistcoat and past a red and blue woolly scarf round the neck, they found themselves looking into a round, shining, kind, wrinkly face, with deep-as-oceans large, brown eyes, and a mass of pure, white, fluffy hair which fell in a tangle over his brow.

'Ah!' exclaimed Grandpa Chatterji with a great, loving sigh, and he opened his arms to embrace them.

After they had all hugged each other, Mum said, 'Children, take Grandpa up to his room, he will want to bath and change after his long journey. I'll go and make a nice cup of tea.'

Sanjay began chattering as he clambered up the stairs, leading the way.

'Why aren't you wearing any shoes?' he asked.

'Because I took them off at the door, so as not to bring any dirt into the house. We always do that in India,' answered Grandpa Chatterji.

'Did you come with lots of suitcases, Grandpa?' Sanjay went on, 'and did you bring us lots of presents?'

'Ssh!' said Neetu, embarrassed. 'That's rude, Sanjay.'

'Just you wait and see,' replied Grandpa, who didn't mind at all.

When they went into the guest room, they couldn't see any suitcases at all.

'Where is your luggage?' asked Neetu.

'Oh, I only ever travel with my bedroll,' said Grandpa. 'My needs are very simple,' and he pointed to a roly-poly round khaki, canvas roll, all held together with leather straps, and covered in airline stickers and labels.

'Does that mean we don't have presents?' sighed Sanjay.

'Just you wait and see,' replied Grandpa again.

'You've got the best room in the house,' chattered Sanjay, bravely trying to ignore the mysterious roll which contained everything that Grandpa had brought.

'You've got the nicest sheets with duvet and curtains to match, you have the plumpiest pillows and the softest bed. It's the best bed in the house for bouncing on,' and Sanjay flung himself on to the bed, which Mum had made all smooth and neat, and he rumpled it all up.

'Sanjay!' cried Neetu with horror, dragging him off. 'Look what you've done,' and she tried

to straighten it out.

'If you like this bed so much, you'd better sleep
in it,' said Grandpa Chatterji. 'I prefer something
harder.'

'Where will you sleep then, Grandpa?' asked
Neetu looking worried.

'I'll sleep on the floor as I always do,' he
replied. 'I am like a snail, my dear,' murmured
Grandpa. 'All I need, wherever I go, is my

bedroll. It carries all my belongings, and when I unroll it, it becomes my bed.'

The children looked in awe at the khaki, canvas roll. It suddenly seemed to be the most important thing in the world. 'Can we unroll it, Grandpa?' whispered Sanjay.

Grandpa bent over the roll and undid the old leather straps, then he slowly unrolled it alongside the bed. At first it seemed that all it contained was one sheet and one blanket. Sanjay was sure there were no presents; but then Grandpa wriggled his hand into the large pocket at one end of the roll and pulled out a tooth mug and toothbrush all wrapped in a towel, a hair brush and comb and his shaving things. Sanjay stared expectantly. Were there any presents?

Then Grandpa went to a pocket at the other end and wriggled his hand inside. He pulled out a woolly jumper, a woolly hat, some socks, underwear, hankies, a shirt, tunic and waistcoat, but still no presents.

At last, he folded back the sheet. Between the sheet and the blanket was a small, faded rug. He pulled back the rug to show lots of different packages.

'Presents!' breathed Sanjay, full of expectation.

'Why did you bring that old rug?' asked Neetu in a puzzled voice.

Grandpa Chatterji lifted it out as though it were the most precious thing in the world. 'I never go anywhere without this,' he murmured. 'It is my meditation rug. I sit on it to do all my thinking and praying.'

'Are those things presents?' asked Sanjay, pointing to the packages.

'Yes, yes, here you are,' laughed Grandpa. He handed Sanjay two long thin packages.

'Thank you, thank you!' yelled Sanjay, ripping them open. 'What are they?'

19

'One is a specially made, wooden wriggly snake, and the other is an Indian flute. Later I will teach you some tunes, but for now, you can just blow. It makes a lovely sound. Snakes love the sound of the flute. It makes them sway and puts them into a good mood.'

Sanjay flung his arms round his old grandfather. 'Thank you, thank you, Grandpa Chatterji!' and he rushed off to show his mum and dad.

Neetu waited patiently. Which package was for her? He bent over and handed her one of the larger ones. 'What a beauty you are, my dearest, little granddaughter! This is for you.'

When Neetu opened up her package, she found a beautiful pink and green and gold sari. It was a special small-sized sari for little girls. In India they have to wait until they are nearly grown-up before they can wear a sari, but all little girls love to have a sari they can dress up in, and this is what her grandfather had brought for her.

It made Neetu feel very solemn and proud. 'Oh thank you, Grandpa!' she declared in a grown-up voice, 'I'll go and ask Mum to help me put it on.'

Later, when Grandpa Chatterji had bathed and changed, Neetu, all dressed up in her sari, and Sanjay, with his snake and flute, went upstairs to

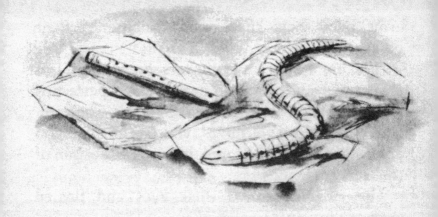

find him. They knocked on his door.

'Come in!' he said in his soft, high voice.

They went in. Grandpa was sitting on the floor on his old rug. He was sitting very straight, his eyes staring in front and his arms stretched over his cross-legged knees.

'What are you doing, Grandpa?' asked Sanjay.

'I'm being a lotus flower floating quietly on a sea of milk.'

'Why are you being a lotus flower?' asked Neetu. She was looking like such a beautiful, grown-up lady in her new sari.

Grandpa looked at her and smiled with admiration. 'Come, children. Come and sit next to me. There's room on the rug.'

Neetu and Sanjay sat cross-legged one on each side of their grandfather. They stretched out their

21

arms over their knees and straightened their backs.

'We are being lotus flowers because we are trying to be as calm and peaceful and perfect as lotus flowers are,' explained Grandpa Chatterji, 'and if you close your eyes, you can imagine you are floating on a sea of milk before the creation of the world.'

The children closed their eyes and floated away.

Then Grandpa suddenly woke up with a shout and cried, 'I feel rested now! Come on! Where's that cup of tea your mother promised me? And while I'm drinking my tea, Sanjay can play the flute, and Neetu can dance! Will you?' he begged, his dark eyes glittering.

Neetu and Sanjay nodded with excitement. 'Oh, Grandpa Chatterji! We're so glad you came.'

2

'Ōm . . . Ōm . . . Ōm . . .'

When Neetu awoke the next morning, the first thing she thought was, 'Did Grandpa Chatterji really sleep on the floor?'

She sat up wide awake. It must be very early, because her room was still dark. Just a faint grey streak of light slipped between the curtains. Outside, the first blackbird had begun his dawn song.

She crept along to Grandpa Chatterji's room. His door was open. She peeped inside. At first she couldn't see anything. Then as her eyes adjusted, she saw that the spare bed, with its flowery duvet, was empty and hadn't been touched. On the floor, rolled out with a flat pillow and blanket was Grandpa Chatterji's bedroll; but there was no sign of Grandpa. Then she heard the sound. A slow, low repeating sound like the throbbing of a fridge, or the wind strumming the telephone wire. Or was it? Neetu listened carefully. Was it her own heart beating? No. Her heart was going boom, boom, boom, like a softly muffled drum. This sound was more like the waves beating against the shore; or a giant breathing . . . or . . ?

Ōm . . . Ōm . . . Ōm . . . The sound seemed to be everywhere; inside and outside. Was it Sanjay playing his flute? She tiptoed out of her bedroom and looked into her brother's room. He

lay fast asleep, sprawled across his bed with his feet sticking out, and an arm flung over his best teddy. His wooden flute lay waiting patiently upon his pillow. Sanjay wasn't making the sound. Was it Dad snoring? She crept into her parents' bedroom. She saw their two humps side by side like bookends under the double duvet. She went closer and stood listening. But no, Mum and Dad were still so deeply asleep that you could hardly hear them breathing at all.

So she went downstairs, past the ticking clock in the hall, past the puff of the boiler as it fired the central heating, past the low throbbing of the fridge and up to the back door. Here, the sound seemed louder. It was coming from the garden. Ōm . . . Ōm . . . Ōm . . . Was it the tree moaning in the wind?

25

She went outside. It wasn't a very big garden. Just a patch of lawn with two long flower beds running the length of the fence on each side. The best thing was the tree at the bottom. It wasn't the sort of tree anyone would plant. Its seed had been blown there by the wind long before Neetu was even born. It had grown quietly and secretly without anybody noticing. It had grown and grown till it was taller than their house. Its branches stretched out like lots of arms, and sometimes the wind blew around it making it creak and swish. It was where the blackbird sang his songs and where the sparrows caused kerfuffles among the clumps of ivy which clung to the trunk. But as Neetu stood outside the back door, she realised that it was a perfectly still morning, with not one breath of wind to even rustle the leaves. Ōm . . . Ōm . . . Ōm . . .

Then she saw him. Grandpa Chatterji was standing at the base of the tree. He wasn't wearing stripy pyjamas as Grandpa Leicester always did. He was bare-footed and was only wearing a thin white cloth wrapped round his waist and a white thread across his bare chest. He had spread out his precious rug, and he stood on one leg with his arms upstretched to the sky, as if he too were part of the tree.

Ōm . . . Ōm . . . Ōm . . . Neetu moved softly. She had nearly called out to her grandfather, but something told her not to. Silently, she walked across the grass and stood at his side. She looked up into his face. It was completely calm. His eyes were open, but he didn't look at her. He didn't even seem to know she was there. He breathed in a long, long breath which expanded his chest, and then he breathed out very very slowly. As he did, the deep, throbbing sound of Ōm soared through the air.

There was just room on the rug for Neetu. Without asking, she stood by his side. She tried to stand on one leg, but wobbled. She tried again, and managed to stand for a little longer. She raised her arms and looked up at the sky. Dawn was breaking through the grey branches, creating islands of pink clouds. Ōm . . . Ōm . . . She copied.

After a while, Grandpa Chatterji looked down at his granddaughter and smiled.

'What are we doing, Grandpa?' she whispered.

'We're praying to God and welcoming a new day. When you make a round shape with your lips and say "O" you are making the shape of the sun, the shape of the world and the shape of the universe. When you make the sound "Ōm" you

are talking to the Creator of Everything.'

Then suddenly, Grandpa stopped being holy.

'I'm starving!' he cried. 'Let's make *pooris*!' He seemed to fly down the garden and into the kitchen. Neetu had to run to keep up.

'Where's the flour?' he asked.

Neetu found the flour.

'Where's the cooking oil?'

Neetu found the cooking oil.

'Where's the mixing bowl?'

Neetu found the mixing bowl.

'Where's the rolling pin?'

Neetu found the rolling pin.

Then Grandpa Chatterji put down his rug on the floor in a corner of the kitchen and began to mix the dough.

Sanjay came in playing his flute. He was still in his pyjamas and his eyes were sticky with sleep.

'Where have you been? I was looking everywhere for you,' he grumbled.

'Grandpa and I were saying hello to the sun,' explained Neetu. 'Look! We stood like this.'

Neetu stood on one leg with her arms up above her head. She breathed in deeply, and as she breathed out, she went 'Ōm . . .'

'That's easy!' scoffed Sanjay. 'I can do that!'

But when he tried, he wobbled all over the place.

'Come and help me with the *pooris*, you two!' interrupted Grandpa. 'Look! I've kneaded the dough. Now you take a handful and work it round into a ball. Then flatten it out on this wooden board and roll it into a circle with the rolling pin. I'll heat up the cooking oil.'

When the oil was smoking hot, one by one, Grandpa dropped the rolled out circles of dough into the sizzling pan.

'Look!' cried Neetu excitedly. 'Look how they puff up!'

'They're just like little footballs!' yelled Sanjay.

'They're round like Ōm,' said Neetu.

Soon they had a plate piled high with *pooris*.

Grandpa had boiled a kettle and made a big pot of tea. He said, 'Let's take your mother and father tea and *pooris* in bed!'

Neetu and Sanjay carried a plate each of *pooris* while Grandpa put five mugs of steaming hot tea on the tray. Then in procession, they climbed the stairs.

Mum and Dad sat up in amazement when they all trooped into the bedroom.

'*Garam Chai*!' announced Grandpa. 'Hot tea!'

'And *pooris* which we made!' boasted Sanjay!

'It's just like being back in India,' sighed Mum.

'These were always your mum's favourite when she was a little girl,' smiled Grandpa Chatterji.

'I think they're my favourite too,' cried Neetu with her mouth full.

Sanjay stood on one leg. He put his hands up above his head, and even though his mouth was full of *pooris*, he said, 'Ōm . . .'

3

Grandpa Rides in a Rocket

They knew the fair was coming to town, because one morning, bright posters were plastered all over the place on walls, in shops. They hung from hooks alongside the legs of lamb in the butcher's and the bunches of bananas in the greengrocers, or they were pinned on to notice boards in public buildings, in the library, in the town hall.

GRAND BANK HOLIDAY FAIR, the posters proclaimed. FUN FOR ALL THE FAMILY; AMUSEMENTS, STALLS, PONY RIDES, THRILLS AND SPILLS AND SPECIAL ATRRACTIONS.

'We must go to that,' said Dad. 'Keep a look out.'

Well, they didn't really need to keep a look out. You couldn't miss it. One day, all the roads through the town were clogged with battered cars

and vans, trailers and caravans, lorries and trucks. Clowns with silly faces mingled with the shoppers and thrust leaflets into their hands; a girl walked by on stilts, ten feet high, waving and smiling.

'I'd like to do that,' sighed Neetu.

When they went home and told Grandpa Chatterji about the fair, his eyes gleamed with pleasure. 'I love fairs,' he beamed. 'I love watching all the elephants and camels and horses and bullock carts, and all the women in their glittering skirts and saris, and all the men wearing their most colourful turbans. Oh good, oh good!' And he rubbed his hands together in anticipation.

'But, Grandpa,' exclaimed Sanjay in a puzzled voice, 'fairs here aren't like that.'

'You're thinking of an Indian fair,' laughed Mum. 'This will be quite different.'

'Oh!' said Grandpa, looking rather downcast. 'What will this fair be like?'

'It will have dodgem cars and merry-go-rounds and waltzers and a ghost train. It will have lots of stalls with games and competitions. I won a fluffy cat last year. I guessed the right number when I tossed in a coin,' Neetu told him.

'Grandpa, will you go on the rockets with me?'

begged Sanjay. 'Everyone else is too scared.'

'I'll go on anything,' boasted Grandpa, looking excited again.

'You'll remember your age, Pa, that's what you'll do,' said Mum firmly.

But Grandpa Chatterji couldn't remember his age. He was ageless. Sometimes he seemed as old and as wise as the universe, and other times, it was as though he had only just been born and had come into the world full of wonder. Now, he looked forward to the fair with all the excitement of a child. He rushed about saying, 'Come on, then. Let's go, let's go! What are we waiting for?'

'We'll go when its dark, Grandpa. It's much more fun,' they told him.

As soon as it was dark, the nearby playing fields were ablaze with light and loud music pulsated through the air. It was magic. No one could resist it. Everyone filled their pockets with money, and soon, all the roads leading to the fair were thronging with families. Mum, Dad, Grandpa, Neetu and Sanjay joined the crowds. Grandpa kept hopping up and down, his eyes wide as saucers. 'Look! Look!' He pointed at glittering machines which lit up the sky as bright as a city. He looked at the giant Rocket Ride, which rose up into the night like a space station, its rockets orbiting and spinning like shooting stars. 'Let's see it all!' cried Grandpa Chatterji.

He was like a moth attracted by the fiery brightness. Not only were there garlands of fairy lights looped from stall to stall all bobbing about in the evening breeze, but there were the more powerful patterns of light from the different machines, which flashed on and off in rhythm to the thundering music. The music was so loud, they could hardly hear themselves speak.

But this wasn't a place for speaking. This was a place for looking and listening and doing. Everyone communicated in sign language. Children held out empty palms to be filled with

coins; they pointed at ice creams, hot dogs or candy floss, and the only human sounds which could be heard, were the high-pitched screams coming from the Ghost Train or the Rocket Ride, as people were whirled round and round, higher and higher, faster and faster.

Grandpa kept rushing over to the different attractions shouting, 'I want to try this! I want to try that!' And he disappeared from sight for minutes on end. They would find him at the Rifle Range, or trying to hook a wrist watch with a fishing line; or tossing darts at playing cards in the hope of winning a huge, pink teddy bear.

The longest time he was out of sight, was when he went into the fortune-teller's tent to have his palm read. Mum and Dad looked everywhere, trying at the same time to keep track of Neetu and Sanjay.

'Can't you keep your father in order?' Dad said to Mum in exasperation.

Then just when they thought they had lost him for good, he emerged from the tent with a smug grin on his face. 'I went in to have my fortune told,' he shouted, 'but it was I who told the fortune-teller's fortune. She's a fraud. She didn't know anything. All she could say was, you have been on a long journey. Then I took her hand,

40

and told her that she had just moved house; her husband had a new job and her daughter had just given birth to twins. She was astounded.'

'Was it true?' asked Neetu.

'Of course it was true,' retorted Grandpa. 'I know what I'm doing.'

'I want to go on the Rocket Ride,' shouted Sanjay.

'No!' said Mum and Dad together. 'You can't go alone, and none of us will go with you.'

'Grandpa would,' said Sanjay, looking slyly up at Grandpa.

Grandpa Chatterji opened his mouth . . . but Dad whisked Sanjay away. 'Look! We're right near the Dodgem Cars. You like those.'

'Oh, yes! Let's go on the Dodgem Cars!' cried Sanjay. He showed Grandpa the little red, yellow and blue cars which raced round dodging and bumping into each other.

'I can't drive!' cried Grandpa.

'Neither can I!' laughed Sanjay, 'but it doesn't matter. All you do is press a pedal and steer.'

'Come on then! Let's go!' cried Grandpa eagerly. 'I've always wanted to drive a car!'

They all went on the Dodgem Cars, even Mum and Dad. Everyone had two goes, except Grandpa, who had three. He would have stayed

on them all night. He was like a demon driver, hurtling around, crashing and bumping, twisting and turning. But in the end, Neetu dragged him off so that he would go with her on the Waltzer.

Grandpa looked back wistfully at the Dodgem Cars. 'Do you think it's too late for me to learn to drive?' he asked.

'Much too late,' said Dad firmly.

On the way to the Waltzer, they passed the Rocket Ride. 'Please come on the Rocket with me, Grandpa!' begged Sanjay!

'No, Sanjay!' protested Neetu. 'Grandpa's coming with me on the Waltzer.'

Grandpa stopped for a moment and looked at the great steely arms of the machine, and the shining silver rockets fixed to the ends. They soared up into the sky, spun around and then dipped down at great speed. It looked so exciting.

'Take me! Take me!' begged Sanjay.

'Look's exciting,' murmured Grandpa. 'I'd like a go on that.'

'Oh no you won't,' Mum yelled as sternly as she could above the din. 'You're too old and Sanjay's too young.'

'Hmm!' snorted Grandpa, and carried on with Neetu to the Waltzer.

So they whirled about on the Waltzer. Then they went on to the Helter-Skelter, sliding down on cushions and landing in a tumble at the bottom. They stumbled round the Funnyhouse laughing at themselves in the distorted mirrors, and they frightened themselves silly in the Ghost Train, screaming until their throats were sore.

When Mum said finally, 'It's time to go home,' everyone groaned – especially Grandpa.

'Must we?' he wailed.

'Really, Pa, you're as bad as the children!' grumbled his daughter.

'I know, I know!' Grandpa hung his head like an old crow, though his eyes never stopped glittering. 'But there's no harm. It's good to be young, even when you're old.'

On their way out, they passed the great Rocket Ride. Grandpa stopped again, and looked at the gleaming rockets, whirling through the night sky. He couldn't resist. 'I cannot leave Great Britain without going on a Rocket Ride!' he exclaimed seriously. I want to go on the Rocket.'

'Me too, Grandpa!' shrieked Sanjay. 'Me too. Mum, you said I could if I found an adult willing to take me, and Grandpa's an adult, isn't he?'

'I wonder, sometimes,' muttered Dad.

'What did you say?' asked Sanjay.

'I said . . .' Dad faltered . . . 'Yes, he's an adult, I suppose.'

'That's settled then. We will go on the Rocket, my boy!' Grandpa Chatterji beamed. Suddenly, Grandpa had decided to act as head of the family. No one could really say no to him once he had made up his mind, not even Mum and Dad. 'Don't worry, daughter,' he reassured Sanjay's mother. 'We'll be fine. We'll hang on to each other for safety, won't we!'

Sanjay laughed triumphantly, and holding Grandpa's hand, they excitedly joined the queue for the next Rocket Ride.

'Neetu, Mum and I will go on the Beetle-Bug Ride while you two make yourselves sick,' said Dad, shrugging with defeat. 'Let's meet here afterwards.'

They all agreed and then separated.

Sanjay looked at the shining bodies of the rockets. They didn't look scary at all from the ground.

'I don't see what's so frightening about those rockets,' cried Grandpa. 'What's all the fuss about?'

'I don't know,' answered Sanjay innocently, although he knew that even his best friend, who was such a toughie, had been scared out of his wits when he went on it last year, and had said he would never go again.

They studied people's faces as the Rocket came to a standstill and the people clambered out. It's true, not many were smiling. Some looked quite green and grim. But no one would admit it had been horrible. Grandpa and Sanjay heard voices saying, 'Phew, that was terrific, wasn't it?' And others replying, 'Yeh! It was really great!'

Grandpa and Sanjay chose a rocket for themselves. They climbed inside and strapped the seat belts on. A man came round collecting the

money, and then when all the rockets had filled up, slowly, slowly, the machine began to move.

At first it started gently. They could look out and see all the people down below.

'Look! There's Neetu and Mum and Dad queuing for the Beetle-Bug Ride.' Sanjay waved frantically, but within a second they were gone, as the Rocket turned, and next time round, they were already too high to make out anybody.

They were only in the Rocket for three minutes, but it was three minutes of hell. Within twenty seconds, they were rotating at a great height, and then the steel arms dipped them down at great speed, so that they were sure they would be tossed into eternity, before it whisked them up again. By the time one minute was up, Sanjay had his face buried in Grandpa's shoulder, whimpering with terror as they were spun about and tipped and somersaulted.

Grandpa shut his eyes. It would have been possible to think that nothing had upset him, except that the knuckles of his fingers were white, as he gripped the arms of his seat.

'Get me off, get me off!' shrieked Sanjay.

But there was no getting off. At last, after two and a half minutes, the Rocket began to slow down bit by bit and gradually drop lower and lower.

When it finally came to a standstill, Grandpa and Sanjay were frozen with shock and didn't get out.

'Having another go, are you?' asked the man holding out his hand for more money.

'Oh no! No!' gulped Grandpa. 'We're going, we're going!'

The whole world was still tipping and turning, as they got out of the Rocket and wobbled their way to the exit. They waited, silent with dizziness, until at last Mum, Dad and Neetu came bounding over. They had had a wonderful ride on the Beetle-Bug.

'Oh, Grandpa! You must go on it!' cried Neetu. 'Come with me now, I'd love another go.'

'No, no!' groaned Grandpa, 'I couldn't manage another ride.'

'Are you two all right?' asked Mum peering at them closely. 'Was it good?'

'It was great!' said Sanjay in a dull voice. He felt sick.

'I've never had such an experience,' said Grandpa, swaying slightly.

'Hmm,' said Dad with a knowing look. 'You both look a bit green. I think it's time we went home.'

Mum popped Sanjay and Neetu into the bath and quickly got them ready for bed. Then she said, 'Just go and say "good night" to Grandpa.' They went downstairs, but Grandpa wasn't watching television with Dad, so they said good night to Dad, and went back up. They went to Grandpa's room and knocked on the door.

'Come in,' said a soft voice.

When they opened the door, there was Grandpa upside down, standing on his head on the rug.

'Oh, Pa! Haven't you had enough of being upside down for one night!' laughed Mum.

'I stand upside down so that I can feel the right way up,' smiled Grandpa.

'Good night, Grandpa Chatterji,' said Neetu bending down on her knees so that she could give her grandfather a kiss.

'Good night, Grandpa Chatterji,' said Sanjay, pressing his mouth close to his grandfather's ear. 'Shall we go back tomorrow and have another ride on the Rocket?' he whispered.

'Perhaps, when I come to England next time,' answered Grandpa weakly, and shut his eyes.

'Good night, then,' they all said again as they reached the door.

Grandpa Chatterji wriggled his feet in the air.

4

When Grandpa Leicester came to stay

Mum was scurrying about. Dad was fiddling with his tie. He always fiddled with his tie when he was nervous. Neetu and Sanjay looked a little solemn. Today Neetu was wearing a dress and Sanjay was wearing grey trousers and a jacket.

Grandpa Chatterji was still only wearing his *dhoti*. He had done his yoga exercises, he had bathed, he had cleaned his teeth, he had washed out his mouth and nose and throat by gargling and snorting with salt water, and he had said his prayers.

When he came down to breakfast, his face was shining with cleanliness and good humour, and he was surprised to notice that everyone looked a little glum.

'What is happening?' he asked. 'Why the long faces?' He looked at his grandchildren. 'Is

50

something wrong?'

'Didn't you know?' cried Neetu. 'Grandpa Leicester is visiting us today! You'd better get dressed.'

'I am dressed,' corrected Grandpa Chatterji.

'Grandpa Leicester will call you "jungly" if you don't put on a suit,' said Neetu doubtfully.

'Don't worry, Grandpa Leicester won't find anything wrong with me when we meet,' replied Grandpa Chatterji, reassuringly.

'I must start preparing food,' murmured Mother. 'Grandpa Leicester is rather fussy about what he eats.' Anxiously, she hurried away.

Soon a smell of cooking drifted through the house. Sanjay screwed up his nose. 'Oh, no! We'll have to eat Grandpa Leicester's favourite food.'

'I'll go and help your mother with the cooking,' said Grandpa Chatterji. 'Maybe I can produce something that you will like, and Grandpa Leicester will like too.'

'Is there room for me in the kitchen?' he asked his daughter.

'There isn't very much space,' she answered warily. 'How many gas rings do you need?'

'One will do!' replied Grandpa Chatterji. He put on a large apron which looped round his neck and covered him from his neck down to his knees. Then he got out a chopping board, and a mixing bowl and a packet of *gram* flour. He found three large onions, garlic, potatoes, cauliflower, carrots, tomatoes, pepper, salt and two or three packets of yellow, brown and orange powder.

Bit by bit, Grandpa spread and spread. Soon he had taken over the whole kitchen. The table and every bit of worktop was covered with something, and each time Mum moved in one direction, Grandpa shifted her to another. She was in despair.

'Too many cooks spoil the broth, Father!' she told him. 'Why don't you leave me to get on with it now?'

But Grandpa Chatterji said, 'Don't take any notice of me. I won't get in your way,' and he carried on with his preparations.

But Grandpa did get in her way, and stubbornly refused to go. Finally, Mum clutched her head. 'There's no room for me to mix my spices. There's no room for me to prepare my spinach and ladies fingers. In fact there's no room for me at all! Either you go or I must go!' she declared. 'There's no room for both of us!'

'Why don't you leave it to me. Relax, have a bath, and put on your best sari,' suggested

Grandpa Chatterji soothingly. 'Leave the food to me!'

Mum shrugged with defeat and fled. 'Don't blame me if the meal is ruined and Grandpa Leicester never comes here again!' she wailed to her husband.

Neetu and Sanjay peeped into the kitchen.

'Grandpa's doing the cooking!' exclaimed Neetu.

'I don't think I'm going to like what Grandpa cooks,' whispered Sanjay, looking suspiciously at the different ingredients. 'I only really like pizza and chips.'

'You liked my *pooris*,' reminded Grandpa, whose sharp ears had picked up Sanjay's words.

'You didn't put hot peppery stuff in your *pooris*,' answered Sanjay.

'I promise I'm not going to make this hot either,' smiled Grandpa, 'but it will be tasty, so tasty, that you'll gobble them all up. Now then, I need a hand. All these vegetables need washing and chopping up. I want the potatoes and carrots diced into small chunks; I want the cauliflower broken into little flowers and someone is going to have to slice the onions.

'I'll do it!' shouted Neetu eagerly.

'I'll do it!' yelled Sanjay.

The kitchen came alive with smells. Smoke and steam poured out through the doors and windows. Grandpa chopped and sliced and tossed and fried and rolled. A big saucepan of fat smoked to boiling point on the gas ring. A large mixing bowl full of batter stood nearby all lumpy with chopped up vegetables. Grandpa was just about to ladle out a portion of batter and drop it, sizzling into the fat, when the doorbell rang.

'Oh, no!' exclaimed the children, 'Grandpa Leicester has arrived already!'

They peeped into the hall and saw Dad opening the front door. 'Father! It's you!' came his voice. 'You're early. We weren't expecting you so soon.'

They saw Grandpa Leicester standing there so smart and stern. He wore a dark grey pinstriped suit; he wore a pure white French shirt with a stiff collar and cuffs which showed exactly two inches beneath the sleeve of his jacket; he had on his smart Rotary Club tie, and on his feet were shiny, mirror-bright black Italian leather shoes.

'Look!' hissed Sanjay. 'Grandpa Leicester's come in his new Jaguar. Do you think he'll take us for a ride?' He stared longingly beyond his grandfather to the beautiful, sleek, low, dark-green saloon car which crouched in the road.

'Shouldn't think so,' muttered Neetu. 'Not after you went and got chocolate all over the seats of his last car.'

They heard Mum coming downstairs, swishing and tinkling. She had put on one of her best saris and wore her bangles and earrings. Grandpa Leicester remarked admiringly, 'Oh, don't you look lovely, my dear!'

'Welcome, *Papaji*!' Mother murmured. 'I do hope you had an uneventful journey.'

'Well! Where is everybody? Where is Chatterji *sahib*?' Grandpa Leicester demanded, stepping inside. 'And where are my grandchildren?'

Neetu stared in horror at Sanjay and pulled him back inside the kitchen. 'Look at you!' she gasped.

Sanjay stared at Neetu. 'Look at you!'

Then they both looked at Grandpa Chatterji. 'Look at Grandpa!' Grandpa Chatterji had yellow batter plastered all up his arms to his elbows, Sanjay looked like a clown, with his hair covered in flour, and blobs of batter on his nose and cheeks; and as for Neetu, she had red eyes running with tears from slicing onions, and her best dress was streaked with masala powders.

'We can't go out and meet Grandpa Leicester

like this!' they cried.

'They'll be here in a minute.' They could hear Mum answering Grandpa Leicester, in a flustery voice. 'Come into the living room and relax. Let me bring you a cup of . . .'

'Aaaachoo!' Sanjay sneezed. He had got flour up his nose.

Grandpa Leicester immediately strode to the kitchen and flung open the door. 'So, my little ones! You are hiding in here, are you?' he cried jovially, then stopped with astonishment. There before him stood Grandpa Chatterji, Neetu and Sanjay all covered in batter and flour looking like white ghosts, and wishing that, like spirits, they could disappear.

If there was one thing Grandpa Leicester couldn't bear, it was mess. They could tell by the critical way his eyes swept around, that he could see nothing but mess; messy children, messy kitchen and a messy Grandpa Chatterji. With sinking hearts, they waited to hear his severe voice telling them off. 'I don't like my grandchildren to look messy.'

Mum looked as if she wished she could disappear through the floor. 'Sanjay! Look at your best jacket and trousers! Neetu! Look at the state of your beautiful dress! Oh, Pa! How could

you let these children get into such a mess?' she
accused Grandpa Chatterji.

'We've been cooking,' exclaimed Grandpa
Chatterji, undaunted. Then he strode up to
Grandpa Leicester with a broad, beaming face and
clasped him in his arms. 'How good to see you
again!'

'Hey, hey!' cried Grandpa Leicester, aghast,
and pulled himself away from Grandpa Chatterji's
floury embrace. 'Oh, no! Look at my best suit!'

Everyone stared in horror at the white imprints
of hands on each of Grandpa Leicester's dark,
pinstriped shoulders.

Mum grabbed Neetu and Sanjay and fled upstairs.

'Ma,' whispered Neetu fearfully. 'What will Grandpa Leicester do to Grandpa Chatterji?'

'I don't know,' she answered in a shaky voice. 'Perhaps he'll just go home again.'

Alone together in the kitchen, the two grandfathers faced each other. Grandpa Leicester opened his mouth to growl a protest at the state of his suit, but no words came out. Grandpa Chatterji tipped his head on one side and smiled like an angel. Then he grabbed Grandpa Leicester by the arm, putting more floury imprints on his sleeves, and pulled him over to the cooker, murmuring sweetly, 'Don't worry about your suit! It will all brush off. Because you are the honoured guest, you must be the first to taste one of my very best *pakoras*. I have made them specially for you.'

Grandpa Chatterji ladled up some batter and dropped it into the smoking oil. There was a sizzling and a splattering and a squealing, as the batter made a golden brown crispy shell all around the vegetables. Grandpa Chatterji dropped in another and another, and soon the pan was bobbing with *pakoras*. As each one was done, he scooped it out with a spatula and dropped it on to a plate covered with a paper towel.

'Eat, eat!' he urged, thrusting the plate under Grandpa Leicester's nose. 'Tell me if you have ever tasted a better *pakora*!'

'Ow!' yelled Grandpa Leicester, as some fat spat on his skin. 'Leave me alone! I'm not hungry yet. I'd rather wait for the proper meal.'

'Oh, but I just want you to test it for me. Tell me if it needs more salt or more *masalas*!' insisted Grandpa Chatterji.

If it had been anyone else in the world, Grandpa Leicester would already have marched out of the kitchen, exploding with anger at the state of his best suit. But somehow, Grandpa Chatterji looked him in the eye with his round, dark, deep-as-oceans eyes, and held the plate so close to his nose that the smell of the *pakora* went straight up his nostrils and made his mouth water.

Grandpa Leicester couldn't resist. 'Oh, all right,' he grunted reluctantly, and popped the *pakora* into his mouth.

'Ah, ah, ah!' he hopped up and down with his mouth open. The *pakora* was piping hot. He flapped his hand in front of his mouth, gradually chewing off little bits and swallowing them. They were delicious. With difficulty, he continued to frown, as if he were still furious about his suit, but the taste of Grandpa Chatterji's *pakoras* was so delicious that, instead of shouting with anger, he ate up all the *pakoras* and held out the plate for more. Gradually his frowns gave way to blissful smiles.

'They're delicious. The best I've ever had. How did you do it? Show me!' He bent over the bowl of batter and watched carefully how Grandpa Chatterji ladled the batter into the oil.

'We need some more vegetables!' cried Grandpa Chatterji. 'Children?' He looked around for Neetu and Sanjay. 'Oh, dear, my assistants have gone. Here!' he thrust a knife into Grandpa Leicester's hand. 'Chop up some more onions, spinach, potatoes and carrots for me while I boil some eggs.'

Time passed. The two grandfathers were still in the kitchen behind closed doors. Neetu and Sanjay had cleaned themselves up and changed their clothes; Dad sat uneasily in the living room, while Mum paced up and down imagining that lunch would be a total disaster.

'When are we going to eat?' moaned Neetu.

'I'm starving!' groaned Sanjay.

Suddenly, the two grandfathers appeared in the doorway. Grandpa Chatterji was still in his *dhoti*

with an overall on top, and Grandpa Leicester –
everyone looked in amazement at Grandpa
Leicester. He had taken off his pinstriped jacket,
removed his smart Rotarian tie and rolled up the
sleeves of his sparkling white French shirt. Most
incredible of all, he had tied a frilly pinny round
his waist.

'Lunch is served!' they both exclaimed
beaming with delight.

What a feast the two grandfathers had
prepared. The table was overflowing with food.
There were bowls of *pakoras*, plates of *pooris*,
tureens of turmeric-coloured lentils and dark

green spinach. There were casseroles of vegetables and egg curries, saucers of pickles, dishes of yogurt and chopped cucumber, and platters piled high with snow-white rice.

'Eat, eat!' begged the grandfathers, passing round the plates.

Everybody ate. Nobody really spoke, except to exclaim, 'Delicious! Wonderful! Can I have another *pakora*? You two should open a restaurant!'

Grandpa Chatterji was right. Even though there was no pizza and chips, everybody found something they liked eating – even Sanjay.

They seemed to eat all afternoon till there was barely a dish which hadn't been scraped clean. Then Mum, Dad and the children said they would do the washing up.

Grandpa Leicester stuck his thumbs in the waist of his trousers and said, 'I've eaten too much and my trousers are too tight.' Then he looked enviously at Grandpa Chatterji. 'I do like your *dhoti*. It's years since I wore one.'

'I have a spare one in my room,' beamed Grandpa Chatterji. 'Please come up and put it on.'

When the children had finished helping in the kitchen they went looking for their grandpas. The house was strangely quiet. Where were they? Perhaps they were snoozing in front of the television; but there was no one in the living room. Perhaps they were sitting in the garden; but there was no one in the garden.

They went upstairs. Grandpa Chatterji's bedroom door was a little ajar. Neetu and Sanjay quietly peered inside. Then they looked at each other and hunched their shoulders in secret laughter. Grandpa Leicester had taken off his uncomfortable pinstriped suit, his French shirt and his Rotarian tie. He had taken off his stiff, shining black leather Italian shoes. His chest was bare and his legs and feet were bare. All he wore was a thin cotton *dhoti*, and he sat cross-legged next to Grandpa Chatterji on his special Indian carpet. Their eyes were shut and their faces were serene and they breathed in for a very long time . . . and out for a very long time.

'What are you doing, Grandpa?' whispered Neetu.

'We're digesting,' said Grandpa Leicester.

'And meditating,' said Grandpa Chatterji.

'When you've finished digesting and meditating, will you take us for a ride in your new Jaguar?' whispered Sanjay tentatively.

'Jaguar?' asked Grandpa Chatterji opening one

eye. 'I've heard of riding *on* an elephant or being pulled *by* a horse, but I've never heard of riding *in* a jaguar.'

'You've never heard of riding in a Jaguar?' asked Grandpa Leicester opening one eye. Then he opened his other eye. 'Shall we take Grandpa Chatterji for a ride in a Jaguar?' he asked his grandchildren with a wink.

'Yes, yes!' shouted the children.

'Have you got any chocolate in your pocket?' asked Grandpa Leicester, sternly.

'No, no!' shouted the children. 'Come on, Grandpa!' and the children grabbed Grandpa Chatterji and Grandpa Leicester and heaved them to their feet.

'There were lots of things I thought I would do when I came to England, but I never thought I would ride in a jaguar!' exclaimed Grandpa Chatterji, somewhat puzzled.

They all went downstairs. They opened the door. There was the Jaguar waiting for them all glossy and shining.

'Ah!' Grandpa Chatterji gave a heartfelt sigh at the beauty of the machine. 'So that is what you call a jaguar! Yes, let's carry on with our digesting in a Jaguar.'

'I think I'd better put on my shoes,' said

Grandpa Leicester. 'I can't drive barefoot.' So he put on his black, shiny, Italian shoes. They looked a little odd with a *dhoti*, but nobody cared. They sank into the soft leathery seats. Grandpa Leicester turned the key. The car roared into life with throbbing power. Then they sped down the road, silent and swift as a jungle cat.

'This is a chariot worthy of the gods!' exclaimed Grandpa Chatterji, overcome with delight. 'It's as good as flying!'

'Ahhah!' agreed Grandpa Leicester, bobbing his head with pleasure. Then he leaned forward to the polished walnut dashboard and opened a compartment. He took out a tin of sweets and passed it to the children in the back of the car. 'You may have one each of these,' he said, so long as they stay in your mouth and you don't get any sticky stuff on my beautiful seats.'

'Oh, thank you, Grandpa Leicester!' cried Neetu, gratefully.

She and Sanjay each popped a sweet into their mouths.

'You know,' Sanjay whispered in Neetu's ear. 'I think I like Grandpa Leicester after all.'

Neetu sucked her sweet and nodded. She caught Grandpa Chatterji looking at her through the rear mirror. He winked. 'I like both our grandpas,' she said, winking back.

5

The Poppy Field

Into the sunshine they stepped. It was a miracle. The air was like silk, sliding softly over their skin. There was a smell of grass and flowers and of earth drying out in steamy vapours rising up and up. The puddles which had glistened in the gutters like dark mirrors, now reflected blue sky; the streets and pavements looked clean and washed.

Grandpa Chatterji shook his head with wonder. Why, only yesterday, he had been so cold, that he had put on his long johns, shirt, three woolly jumpers and two pairs of socks; he had wound a thick woollen scarf round his neck and put a woolly hat on his head which he pulled down right over his ears; and still he had felt cold. That morning, he had tried to say his prayers out in the garden under the tree, standing on one leg to

welcome a new day. But it was so much harder when he was shivery and cold and all bundled up like that. Finally, he had made a hot water bottle and, clutching it tightly to his chest had muttered, 'I'm going back to bed.' Neetu and Sanjay had peeped into his room an hour later. Grandpa had been lying in his bedroll with the blanket pulled up to his chin. Two deep brown eyes had stared miserably at them over the top.

'England is too cold for me!' he had groaned. 'How long will this last?'

The children shook their heads. Who could tell?

Now a sliver of gold burst through the cracks in the curtain, and when they looked outside, there was the sun riding high through the sky and it was as though the world had been created all over again.

'That's more like it!' exclaimed Grandpa, stretching out his limbs to absorb the warmth. But he was still disbelieving. Could the weather change so quickly from cold to hot? So he still put on his long johns, shirt, three woolly jumpers and two pairs of socks; and he still wrapped a scarf round his neck and pulled a woolly cap down over his ears.

'Grandpa? Won't you be too hot?' asked Neetu, looking at his red face.

'Well, perhaps I can take off one of my woolly jumpers,' agreed Grandpa. So he took off one. 'That's better!' he said.

Sanjay saw a trickle of perspiration sliding down Grandpa's cheek from beneath his woolly cap. 'Grandpa, aren't you baking under that hat and scarf?'

Grandpa thought about it. He went outside and put out a hand to test the temperature. Yes, it was a much warmer day. So he removed his hat and scarf. 'That's better,' he said.

Mum came in. She was wearing light cotton trousers and a short-sleeved blouse. Grandpa looked at her doubtfully. 'Aren't you too cold like that? This isn't India.'

'No, Father, this isn't India. This is England, where the weather can change from hot to cold all in one day. You have to be prepared. Yesterday was cold, but today is really warm, much too warm for you to be wearing two pullovers and two pairs of socks and your long johns!'

Grandpa nodded ruefully, and took off another pullover and one pair of socks. 'That's better,' he sighed. 'Now I feel comfortable. Now I feel like a walk.'

He jumped up, suddenly full of energy. 'Come on everybody! Let's go walking! I want to find the poppy field!'

'What poppy field?' asked Neetu and Sanjay.

'What poppy field?' asked Mum and Dad.

No one knew of any poppy field.

'Let's go, let's go,' urged Grandpa. 'I can't come all this way to England and not see a poppy field. I know there's a poppy field. Trust me! We'll find one.'

'But Father,' Mum cried in a mystified voice. 'It's too early for poppies. They come in the summer and it's only April, and in any case, you won't find poppy fields in a town!'

'Come along, come along!' insisted Grandpa. 'I'll show you!'

Mum, Neetu and Sanjay looked at each other and grinned.

'Oh, well! It is Saturday, and there's nothing planned. It's such a nice day, so it won't hurt to go hunting for a poppy field that doesn't exist; and a walk does you good,' agreed Mum. So they followed Grandpa outside.

'Are you coming, dear?' Mum asked Dad before she closed the front door.

'I'm not going on any wild goose chase,' snorted Dad. 'Anyway, I want to watch the cricket on telly.'

'See you later then!' she cried.

'I hope so!' laughed Dad. 'If your father doesn't walk you all the way to Timbukto.'

Grandpa Chatterji strode out ahead with his umbrella in hand. 'Just in case it rains,' he had muttered. 'As you never seem to know where you are in this country!' He stuck the spike out in front of him to point the way.

Mum, Neetu and Sanjay followed behind. Where would Grandpa lead them? They walked down to the end of the road and reached a T-junction. Grandpa stopped and held up his umbrella as if it would somehow tell him which way to go, then he turned smartly right.

'Are we nearly there?' asked Sanjay, beginning to dawdle.

'Just a little further,' replied Grandpa, cheerily.

They walked and walked and walked, passing row upon row of houses. People were working in their gardens or washing the car. Some stopped and waved; and some cried out, 'Where are you going on this nice, fine day?'

'We're going to find a poppy field for Grandpa!' shouted Neetu.

Then the people had shaken their heads in puzzlement. 'This is the town not the country. You won't find a poppy field round here – and anyway, it's the wrong time of year.'

'Never mind,' Mum reassured them. 'It will give us a good walk in the sunshine.'

They came to a small road which they had never walked down before. There was an old grey stone church. It stood in the middle of a triangular churchyard on the corner of a fork in the road. A sleek, black cat crouched in the long, overgrown grass among the tombstones. Grandpa stopped and held up his umbrella. The point swung in one direction, then in another and then back again. The cat watched; the children watched and Mum watched.

'Are we nearly there?' asked Sanjay.

'It can't be far now,' murmured Grandpa encouragingly.

'Which way do we go, Grandpa?' cried Neetu.

'This way, this way!' exclaimed Grandpa confidently, and marched off down the left fork. As if curious to know where they were going, the black cat followed.

They walked and walked and walked.

Then the road suddenly ended. There they were standing in a quiet cul-de-sac, where a semi-circle of little brick houses seemed to be spying on them secretly through their net-curtained windows. The neat gardens formed a lush semi-circle of lawns, bushes, flower beds and trees. The gardens were divided one from the other by a mixture of walls, hedges and fences. They couldn't see any road which would take them further.

'When are we getting there?' moaned Sanjay. It seemed to him that they had walked quite far enough.

'Not long, not long!' cried Grandpa. He lifted up his umbrella. He seemed to be relying on it to lead the way. It turned a vague circle in the air above his head and looked inclined to take them back the way they had come. Grandpa shut his eyes and stood on one leg.

'Are you praying, Grandpa?' asked Neetu.

'Grandpa opened one serious eye and stared down at her. 'I'm thinking,' he answered.

'I'll think with you,' said Neetu, and stood on one leg with her eyes closed.

'Perhaps we should give up now, and go home,' suggested Mum.

'Don't be faint-hearted, my dear! You should know that you can trust your father. Be patient,' he ordered, and closed his eyes again.

So Mum sat on a low wall and admired the pretty gardens while the black cat coiled itself round their legs purring loudly.

Suddenly, the cat darted across the road and sprang on to a wall. It stretched forward on to its front paws spreading out its claws, then backwards. Neetu opened her eyes. She stopped standing on one leg and watched the cat, smiling. It leapt down and disappeared between two gardens.

'That's funny!' thought Neetu. 'Where did it go?' She ran across the road to where the cat had been sitting. Then she saw that it had walked up a narrow little lane, almost hidden between the wall and an overgrown hedge.

'Hey! Look what I've found!' Neetu cried. 'There's a path here.'

Grandpa's umbrella swung in Neetu's direction. 'Good!' he exclaimed. 'That must be the way we have to go.'

It was a narrow, leafy lane, overhung with the branches of trees and trailing ivy. It led them all the way between people's houses and back gardens, until suddenly it came to some steps leading up to a wooden bridge.

'Good heavens!' cried Mum. 'It's brought us to an old railway line.'

Neetu and Sanjay raced up on to the bridge. They peered down through the iron bars. 'This can't be a railway line! There aren't any rails!' cried Neetu.

'Won't we see a train, then?' moaned Sanjay with disappointment. He thought that seeing a train would be much more exciting than finding a poppy field.

'I'm afraid it's a disused track now,' said mother. 'They've turned it into a path for walkers and cyclists.'

'Then that is where we must go,' said Grandpa firmly, and strode across the bridge and down the other side.

The black cat was waiting. It slid through the long grass which wavered across the path. It seemed to know they would come.

'We've lived here for years,' exclaimed Mum, 'and I never knew about this track. I wonder where it goes?'

'To the poppy field, of course!' answered Grandpa, and set off at a rapid pace. The others had to run to keep up.

The railway banks rose steeply on either side, bursting with flowers – all white and yellow and pink and blue. There were parson's lace and ragwort and celandine and campion and clusters of violets and straggles of forget-me-nots, all nodding gently as if talking to each other.

'Which ones are poppies?' asked Grandpa.

'None of these,' stated Mum firmly. 'I told you. Poppies come later.'

'Humm!' snorted Grandpa, disbelievingly, and continued striding ahead.

'I wish I'd brought my bike,' sighed Sanjay.

'We'll come back here again! It's a wonderful place for you to ride bicycles. So safe without any traffic to worry about,' Mum promised him.

'But I want to see Grandpa's poppy field,' cried Neetu, impatiently. 'You do know there is one, don't you, Grandpa? You aren't wrong, are you?'

'Of course I'm not wrong. I'll find a poppy field. Just you see!' Grandpa wagged his finger at them confidently. 'Trust me.'

They saw a round black hole looming ahead. It was like a huge black eye. 'What's that?' gasped Sanjay.

'It's a railway tunnel,' Mum told him.

It looked exciting. Sanjay and Neetu began running towards it. The black cat overtook them and darted ahead.

For a moment, they paused on the edge between bright sunlight, and the black darkness of the tunnel. They could feel the sudden chill on their skin, and their voices echoed strangely. They hesitated and looked back. Mum and

Grandpa were hurrying towards them. They smiled reassuringly, so Neetu and Sanjay ran on inside the tunnel. The black cat stayed back in the sunlight, its fur suddenly standing on end, and its tail stiffening. Then it sprang up the bank into the long grass and disappeared over the top.

Far, far ahead, at the end of the darkness, the children could now see something round and silver gleaming in the distance. 'What's that?' whispered Sanjay. His words echoed round their heads.

Mum's voice answered back softly. 'It's the light at the end of the tunnel!' she chuckled.

Somehow, Sanjay and Neetu no longer wanted to run on ahead. They waited for Grandpa and Mum, and fixing their eyes on the silvery light, they walked together, steadily towards the other end.

Nearer and nearer they went. Nobody spoke, but there was a feeling of magic in the air. They were about to make a discovery. They were almost at the end of the tunnel, when suddenly, just as they were about to step out into daylight, Grandpa stopped dead in his tracks.

'What is it, Father?' asked Mum with alarm.

'It's the poppy field. It's out there. I told you we'd find it,' he breathed.

He closed his eyes and pressed his hands together in front of him with his elbows sticking outwards and did not take another step forwards.

Bursting with excitement, Neetu ran out of the tunnel. She stood, blinded for a few moments by the bright daylight. She looked eagerly around. 'Where are the poppies, Grandpa?' cried Neetu. She ran further up the track looking this way and that. 'I can't see any poppies,' she wailed, her voice rising with disappointment. She ran back to the tunnel. Grandpa was still standing inside.

'Grandpa, you were wrong. There are no poppies here,' she cried accusingly.

'Ssh!' whispered Mum, comfortingly. 'I think Grandpa has his own special eye. He's seeing the poppies in his own mind with his inner eye. If you shut your eyes, perhaps you will see a field of poppies, too.'

Neetu and Sanjay gazed around them. The sloping banks on either side of the railway track were entirely green, with long stems of waving grass, and the black cat stalking across the top. They closed their eyes, and inside their heads, tried to imagine the banks all red with poppies.

Grandpa never came out of the tunnel. He just stood there with his eyes closed. At last, he waved his umbrella and shouted, 'Now I can go back to

India satisfied!' he called.

Neetu and Sanjay looked at their mother, puzzled.

'Can Grandpa see lots of things with his mind's eye?' asked Sanjay.

'I wouldn't be satisfied just seeing it in my mind,' muttered Neetu. 'He could have stayed at home and imagined it there.' She couldn't help feeling let down. She had thought that Grandpa could never be wrong. She really believed he would find a field of poppies.

'Oh, well,' said Mum kindly. 'Let's go home.'

By the time summer came, Grandpa had gone back to India. He wrote them a letter and said, 'I will never forget the beautiful poppies. Perhaps, next time you go back to the railway tunnel, you can pick one for me and press it in a book and then send it to me.'

'But, Mum, there weren't any poppies!' cried Sanjay shaking his head.

'He was just imagining things,' snorted Neetu indignantly.

'Take me to this tunnel. It sounds interesting,' said Dad. 'For once, I feel like a walk.'

'Oh, yes! And this time, can we take our bikes?' begged the children.

'I hope I can remember the way,' murmured Mum. 'Perhaps that black cat will turn up and help us.'

It was a quiet June afternoon. The streets were hushed with an after-lunch sleepiness. The children rode their bikes on the empty pavements. Somehow they easily remembered the way they had walked with Grandpa. They reached the church on the corner. The black cat was sitting on the wall, as if it had been waiting for them all this time. Time wound backwards. Everything happened in the same way. The cat led them down the road to the cul-de-sac and then leapt up the path between the houses. When they reached the steps of the railway bridge, Mum and Dad carried the bikes up and over and down the other side. Once on the track, Neetu and Sanjay mounted again and went pedalling on towards the tunnel as fast as they could. This time, they didn't hesitate when they reached the black opening of the tunnel, but plunged inside. Their laughter echoed on and on.

Now Mum and Dad reached the tunnel entrance. They could see their children's shapes outlined far ahead in the silvery daylight at the other end.

Suddenly they heard a shriek of astonishment. 'Mum! Dad! Look!'

The parents ran. The children stood still in the darkness of the tunnel, as if not daring to go out.

'What is it?' gasped Dad.

Mum stopped as if transfixed, then slowly, she walked out into the sunlight. 'Poppies!' she exclaimed.

The railway banks, which just two months ago had been nothing but thick, long, wavery green grass, were ablaze with blood-red poppies.

'Is this what Grandpa saw in his mind's eye?' asked Neetu in amazement.

'It must be,' whispered Mum. 'I told you he had a special eye.'

Sanjay dropped his bicycle to the ground, and for a while they stood in silent amazement. Then Neetu whispered, 'Shall I pick one for Grandpa?'

'Just one,' said Dad. 'Then when we get home, we'll press it inside our encyclopaedia.'

'Yes, we'll do that!' cried Mum with enthusiasm, 'And later, when it has dried, I'll stick it on to some card and we'll send it to Grandpa in India.'

The poppy dried out in the encyclopaedia, but though it was flattened, it still looked beautiful on its long stem and its whispery leaves, and it was still as red as the day they picked it. Mum carefully stuck the red poppy on to a piece of white card. Inside, she wrote: 'With much love to Grandpa, who took us on a walk and found a field of poppies.'

Then they all signed their names: Mum, Dad, Neetu and Sanjay.

1

Blood Relatives

It was dawn. Up on the flat roof of a house in Calcutta, Grandpa Chatterji sat cross-legged in a lotus position. Although his eyes were closed, inside his head he was watching. He could see his British grandchildren, Neetu and Sanjay excitedly getting ready to come to India to visit him. They dashed to and fro between an open suitcase and a bed full of presents which they were packing to bring to England.

Rahul climbed the stone steps up to the top, and as he stepped out on to the roof, the sun appeared, glinting between the flat leaves of the banana tree like a hard gold coin. He was carrying the photograph album. Quietly, he sat down next to his grandfather and crossed his legs.

'When my cousins come from England, will they bring me a present, Grandpa?' he whispered.

Grandpa smiled. 'What do you hope they will bring?'

'A cricketing outfit!' Rahul said without hesitation.

'Hmm,' murmured Grandpa. He knew his British grandson loved football. Yet maybe . . . Grandpa focused his mind . . .

Rahul opened the album and began to turn the pages. After a while he came to a section full of his British relatives in their English garden.

There was Sanjay in his football kit and there was Neeta in jeans and T-shirt playing on a

skateboard. 'They look very different from us. They don't look like my other cousins,' muttered Rahul.

'Hmmm,' Grandpa grunted thoughtfully. 'In some ways they are different; they wear different clothes, they eat different food and they play different games, but the same blood as yours flows through their veins.'

Rahul held up his hands and looked at the veins which spread like spidery veins in a leaf. How strange to think that people he had never seen, never touched, never ever spoken to, should have the same blood in their veins as he. He took his grandfather's old hand and held it up. He studied the thicker veins which criss-crossed like the spreading branches of a tree, from his knobbly knuckles to his great bony wrists.

'Your mother, and Neetu and Sanjay's mother are my daughters,' explained Grandpa Chatterji. 'They both have my blood in them, and so my blood is in you and your cousins too. We are blood relatives.'

'Blood relatives!' Rahul liked the sound of that. 'Is Vinod a blood relative?' He pointed to a photograph of a little boy standing in a family group at a wedding.

'No, he's just a relative,' said Grandpa. 'He

does not have any of our blood in his veins. He is a relative by marriage. He is your uncle's wife's sister's child!' And Grandpa burst out laughing when he saw Rahul's face screw up with puzzlement as if he were trying to work out a difficult sum. 'But what does it matter?' asked Grandpa, holding Rahul's smaller hand against his big old one. 'We're all part of the same blood of the universe. We all spring from God.'

However, for the rest of the day, Rahul went round trying to work out who was a blood relative and who a relative by marriage – and who were all the people he called aunts and uncles, when they weren't related at all, but just grown-up friends.

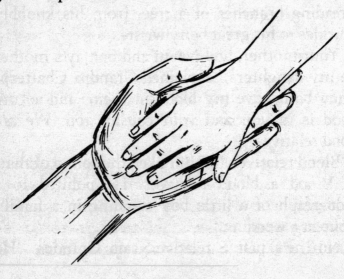

Across the ocean in England Mum said, 'What shall we take for Rahul and Radha?'

'If she's anything like me, then I think Radha would like a very complicated jigsaw puzzle,' said Neetu. 'The harder the better.'

'If he's anything like me, then I think we should take Rahul a football strip and scarf,' said Sanjay. 'He probably loves football.'

That night, Sanjay had a dream. He dreamt that he had arrived in Calcutta and Rahul came rushing up to him laughing. 'Did you bring me a cricketing outfit?' When Sanjay gave him a football strip instead, Rahul ran away shouting, 'I don't like football!'

Sanjay frowned in his sleep. 'How silly! Everyone loves football.'

Sanjay forgot all about his dream till he was in the sports shop with his mother, choosing a football strip for Rahul. They looked at all the colours. Should they take Manchester United, or Everton, or Liverpool or West Ham? He couldn't decide.

'You choose, Mum,' he muttered, suddenly losing interest. He wandered off round the shop. Suddenly he saw a picture of Ian Botham in full cricketing gear; pullover, helmet, gloves, knee-pads, bat and ball. Sanjay stood staring at it.

'Sanjay!' his mother called. 'I've decided on this football strip. Come and see. It's supposed to be a present from you.'

Sanjay didn't answer. He just stood in front of the cricketing picture like a statue.

'Sanjay! Have you gone to sleep?' laughed Mum.

'I had a dream,' murmured Sanjay. Suddenly it all started coming back to him. 'I dreamt that Rahul wanted a cricket outfit. He likes cricket, not football!'

Mum came and stood beside him. 'It's true, that Calcutta is cricket crazy. The whole of India is cricket crazy,' she said thoughtfully.

'Then we must buy him a cricket outfit, just like the one Ian Botham is wearing!' cried Sanjay waking up with a shout. 'I'm sure that's what he would like!'

Mum shrugged and went back to the shop assistant. 'I'm sorry,' she said. 'We've changed our minds. 'We'd like to buy a cricket kit: helmet, pullover, gloves, knee-pads, bat and ball.'

'I hope Radha likes her jigsaw puzzle. I didn't dream that she wanted anything else,' said Neetu.

The day arrived at last. The day Mum, Dad,

Neetu and Sanjay were setting off to visit Grandpa Chatterji in Calcutta.

Mum and Dad were concerned not to forget anything. They kept checking their list: passport, visas, tickets, malaria tablets, water-purifying tablets, tummy pills, mosquito repellent, insect-bite cream . . .

'We seem to be taking the whole chemist's shop,' Dad exclaimed.

'Better safe than sorry,' retorted Mum.

Then there were three suitcases: one for Mum and Dad: one for Neetu and Sanjay and one for the presents, including the jigsaw puzzle for Radha and the cricket kit for Rahul.

That morning, they had to get up very early. Everyone was rushing to and fro. Mr Bolton, their neighbour, had offered to drive them to the airport. They heard the beep of his car.

'Mr Bolton's here! Come on, everybody,' cried Dad.

Down came Mum and Dad's suitcase, down came Neetu and Sanjay's suitcase, and as Mum kept stuffing odds and ends into the hand luggage, Dad helped Mr Bolton stack the car.

Then they all piled in and, at last, they were off.

They had hardly settled down, when Dad began to check everything. 'Have we got the passports? Tickets and visas? Traveller's cheques . . .?'

They drove on a bit further, and Mum was thinking, 'Have we got everything? Malaria tablets, water tablets, mosquito repellent, insect-bite cream . . .'

Rahul sat cross-legged next to his grandfather. High in the sky, they saw a tiny silver speck etching a white line across the dawn sky. It was hard to believe that nearly three hundred people were flying through the air in that speck, which was really a jumbo jet.

'Soon Neetu and Sanjay will be up there,' murmured Grandpa Chatterji, happily.

'My blood relatives,' added Rahul happily, 'and I hope they don't forget to bring us presents.'

Grandpa closed his eyes.

* * *

97

'Did you pack my summer jacket?' asked Dad.

'Yes, but you nearly forgot your blue trousers. Luckily I remembered to get them from the dry cleaner's,' said Mum.

Then Neetu said, 'Have we got the suitcase with the presents?'

'I didn't put it in,' said Mum.

'I didn't put it in,' said Dad.

'I only stacked two suitcases on the roof rack,' said Mr Bolton.

'Oh no!' A terrible groan went up. 'We've forgotten the presents!'

With a jolt of brakes and a screech of tyres, Mr Bolton turned the car round, and they drove back home as fast as they could.

'That was a quick trip to India,' laughed the milkman from his milk float, as he hummed round the neighbourhood.

Dad found the third suitcase under Sanjay's bed. He heaved it on to the roof rack and tied it down. Then off they set again.

After a while, Mum said, 'Have we got everything?'

They went through the check list again: passport, tickets, traveller's cheques, malaria tablets, mosquito repellent . . . *three* suitcases.

* * *

'They won't forget the presents, will they, Grandpa?' asked Rahul.

'No,' smiled Grandpa, getting to his feet and stretching up as high as he could to the sky. Calcutta had woken up. The sounds of honking horns and beeping motor-scooters and roaring buses; cows cawing and imams calling to prayer reverberated all around them. 'No,' said Grandpa with certainty. 'They won't forget the presents.'

2

Where's Grandpa?

'Get up, get up, get up!' Aunty Meena rushed into the children's room. Radha and Rahul were still curled up tightly asleep.

'Come on, come on, come on!' Aunty Meena always liked to talk in threes.

Radha and Rahul groaned.

'Don't you want to be ready for your cousins? They're coming from England today so up, up, up! *Jangra bangra!* Have your baths, do your teeth, get dressed!'

Out in the courtyard, Great Grandma had already been moved into the soft early morning sun. She sat on her string bed covered with a quilt and reached out to give bits of carrot to her pet mynah bird, Hello. He was called Hello because when he first came, that was the only word he knew. Now, after living with the Chatterji family

100

for a while, he knew lots of words and lots of voices, so that sometimes people didn't know whether it was a human speaking or the mynah bird.

Hello flew into the children's bedroom and settled on Radha's head. 'Get up, get up, get up!' he ordered in Aunty Meena's voice.

'Oh, shut up, Hello!' retorted Radha rudely.

'Shuttup, shuttup, shuttup!' repeated Hello.

Then Radha sat up with a jerk. 'Oh, Hello! You naughty boy. You've gone potty potty all over my hair,' and she dashed out of bed, rushed to the bathroom and tossed a jug of water over her head.

'Naughty boy, naughty boy, naughty boy!' agreed Hello.

Outside, the whole of Calcutta was up and about. What a sound of honking, tooting, cheeping, cawing, calling, singing and praying filled the air; and the shrill sound of reed pipes and thudding drums – for it was the season of weddings and processions; but it all seemed to be celebrating the arrival of their cousins from England.

Little Sassu who came to help round the house was already at the courtyard pump filling a pail. She had just turned up one day, asking if they needed help. Grandma Chatterji could see she was poor, so she said that Sassu could peel and chop vegetables, pick stones out of the lentils and sift the rice. But soon, Sassu showed she could do more: she washed the dishes, kneaded the *chapatti* dough and combed Great Grandma's hair. Once a month she would call her uncle from the gate. He was a rickshaw puller. Once a month she would sit like a lady, while her uncle pulled her all the way across the city to see her mother and father and all her brothers and sisters. She would give them her earnings, and then, after staying two nights, her uncle would pull her all the way back again.

'Sassu!' Radha was calling her.

'Sassu!' repeated Hello.

'Please come and plait my hair,' cried Radha.

Sassu came skipping over. She and Radha were friends and often played together.

The milkman called at the gate.

'*Korn?*' demanded Hello in Great Grandma's voice.

As '*Korn*' means 'Who is it?', the milkman called out, '*Doodwallah!* Milk!'

Grandma Chatterji had heard this conversation and bustled out to him carrying her milk pail. 'I'll need extra milk today,' she told him happily. 'My daughter and her family are visiting from England. They arrive today!'

The milkman lifted the huge churn of milk from his head and measured out a cataract of white milk into Grandma's pail.

'It's nearly time to go!' announced Uncle Ashok from the veranda. 'Where's Grandpa?'

'I don't know,' answered Radha, as Sassu oiled her hair till it shone inky black and then deftly divided and plaited it tightly, so that not one strand would stick out.

'I can't see him,' shouted Rahul from the roof where he had gone to fly his kite.

'He didn't come this way,' muttered Aunty Meena as she crouched over the beautiful welcoming *rangoli* pattern she was sprinkling outside the front gate.

'Heaven only knows where Grandpa is,' sighed Grandma Chatterji from the kitchen. She and Laxmi the cook were preparing a special spicy rice and lots of vegetables, ready for their hungry visitors from England.

'Grandpa!' squawked Hello, giving Great Grandma an affectionate nip on her ear.

'It's time to go!' insisted Uncle Ashok, getting agitated. 'Where is Grandpa? We'll be late if we don't leave now!'

They all crowded round the gate, trying not to step on Aunty Meena's *rangoli*. 'I'm gong to hail a taxi,' said Uncle Ashok, 'and if Grandpa doesn't turn up, we'll just have to leave without him.'

He stood on the edge of the pavement, just between the *paan* seller and the pavement barber. Cars and cows and buses and rickshaws all rushed by, but he couldn't see a yellow Hindustan taxi. He looked at his watch and began to feel nervous. 'We're going to be late,' fretted Uncle Ashok. 'I can't see a taxi anywhere. How is it you can never get one when you really need it?'

'I see one!' shouted Rahul.

'Get it, get it, get it!' cried Aunty Meena.

'There's already someone in it,' groaned Uncle Ashok.

'Perhaps it will stop here,' said Radha. 'It's coming this way.'

The yellow taxi came nearer and nearer.

'Taxi, taxi!' yelled the mynah bird.

They couldn't see who was in the taxi. All they could see were flowers.

Then suddenly, a voice rang out, 'Come on, all of you! Get in. We're going to be late!'

'Grandpa!' everyone shouted.

They all piled in, trying not to squash the garlands of marigolds and jasmine and bunches of carnations and lilies.

'Why did you disappear just at the time we had to go?' grumbled Uncle Ashok.

'I had to go to the flower market. We couldn't

greet our guests without flowers!' said Grandpa Chatterji. 'And anyway, I knew there would be taxis to be found there.

It was very crowded at the airport and they had to wait such a long time. As passengers began coming out with all their bags and suitcases, Radha and Rahul looked and looked to see if they could recognise their cousins, as they had only ever seen them in photographs. Then, suddenly, there was a family who looked Indian, but who wore western clothes. The girl and boy were both wearing jeans and trainers and carried sports bags on their shoulders.

'Didi, Didi, Didi!' cried Aunty Meena, rushing towards her older sister. Then what a lot of hugging and kissing and a fierce pinching of cheeks there was. Neetu and Sanjay's mother and father both bent down respectfully and touched the feet of Grandpa and Grandma Chatterji.

'Welcome to Calcutta!' beamed Grandpa, draping their necks with garlands, and thrusting bunches of roses and lilies into his daughter's arms.

Grandpa wanted them all to squeeze into one taxi. He couldn't bear to be parted from any of them, but finally he agreed, two taxis were necessary.

'This is better than Disneyland,' exclaimed Neetu and Sanjay, as the taxis drove at breakneck speed, weaving in and out of the traffic and swerving to avoid cows and dogs and pigs who wandered into the road.

Suddenly, Neetu and Sanjay's taxi began to make funny noises. It began to cough and choke and splutter. It went slower and slower and finally stopped – right in the middle of the road. Horns were hooting and honking: 'Get out of the way!' – but what were they to do?

'I'm sorry,' said the taxi driver. 'My taxi's broken down. It won't go any further. You'll have to find another one.'

'We can all squeeze in with the others,' declared Grandpa Chatterji.

'No – we can't,' groaned Uncle Ashok, but though they stood and stood and waved their arms, another taxi didn't come along.

'We'll have to try and squeeze in,' persisted Grandpa Chatterji. 'We can't stand here all day.'

Then over the roar of the traffic, they heard a little voice calling! 'Radha! Rahul! Are those your cousins arrived from England?'

There, being pulled along by her uncle, was Sassu in a rickshaw.

'I've got a good idea!' exclaimed Grandpa Chatterji rushing over to have a word with Sassu's uncle.

Great Grandma sat on her string bed in the courtyard, listening. She too was full of excitement that her grandchild and great-grandchildren were coming. Her eyes were very bad now, but her ears were sharp. She listened to the sounds in the street outside. She could hear the hawkers shouting their wares, the tring-tring of bicycle bells, dogs barking, crows cawing and the roar of traffic. But her ear was tuned to pick up the sound of an arrival.

She didn't stir when she heard a taxi drawing

up. She didn't move when she heard the voices of excited children thanking Sassu and her uncle for pulling them all the way home in his rickshaw. She just waited patiently, stroking with one finger the sleek black feathers of her pet bird.

Suddenly, Hello hopped excitedly and called out in Great Grandma's voice, *'Korn?'*

Great Grandma looked up. 'Who is it?' she whispered.

Neetu and Sanjay came forward shyly. They touched her feet and embraced her. 'Great Grandma, it's us!'

3

Calcutta Night

Neetu awoke. It was a dark, dark night. She knew she should be asleep, but her body wanted to be awake. Her body thought it was eight o'clock in the morning and time to get up. But her body hadn't yet understood that it was no longer in England; it was in India, and the time was only three o'clock in the morning.

Suddenly her brain was pounding with images and new experiences. She smiled when she remembered how Grandpa Chatterji had introduced them to their cousins, Radha and Rahul.

'Are they blood relatives?' Rahul had demanded.

'The same blood which flows in my veins and your veins also flows in theirs,' Grandpa had answered, and they examined each others hands and then studied each other's faces to see what other things were the same.

'Do you like cricket?' Rahul asked Sanjay.

'Well . . . I prefer football.' Then when he saw Rahul's face drop with disappointment, Sanjay cried, 'but look what we've brought for you!' and he excitedly unpacked the cricket outfit.

'Do you like jigsaws and flying kites?' Radha asked Neetu.

'I've never flown a kite,' said Neetu, 'but look what I've brought for you!' and she gave Radha the very complicated jigsaw with a picture of Big Ben and the Houses of Parliament.

At first, Neetu thought she would be afraid of Grandma Chatterji. Grandma didn't smile as much as Grandpa and she had very piercing, light brown eyes which looked as if they could read your mind. But suddenly, Grandma said softly, 'Here, little granddaughter, here is something for you,' and she slipped into Neetu's hand a little cloth bag, which drew open and closed with a twisty cord and was all stitched with silver threads and mirrors. Inside were ten rupees.

Neetu breathed deeply in and out. Now she was really awake. She could smell the garland of fresh marigolds which Grandpa Chatterji had draped round her neck at the airport. She hadn't

taken it off for the rest of the day, and before
getting into bed, she had hung it on the bedpost
near her head. Its perfume mingled with the
sweet lotus scent of the incense sticks which
burned in the *puja* room.

The *puja* room. Neetu shivered with awe as she
thought of the strange inhabitants in that room.
Three small figures dressed in silks and adorned
with tiny garlands of jasmine and rosebuds stood
on an altar. The figures were gods: there was the
goddess Laxmi, who was the bringer of good
fortune, the elephant-headed god Ganesh, who
was the bringer of wisdom and the remover of
obstacles, and there was the dancing figure of
Lord Shiva, the destroyer of all evil. On a wall

was a gold-framed picture, also garlanded. It was a picture of Rama and Sita – the god prince and goddess princess who had fought such battles with Ravanna, the king of the demons. But it was as though the gods were alive. The family dressed them, fed them and cared for them and, every day, they prayed to them. Before supper that night, Radha showed Neetu how they took a little bit of food from every dish and placed it before the gods in the *puja* room. 'Feed God then feed self,' she told her.

As Neetu lay in her bed, she wondered if those statues came alive; if Shiva danced through the darkness, waving his six arms and killing demons; if Laxmi smiled at what a beautiful *rangoli* pattern Aunty Meena had made, to please her, as well as the relatives from England, and if good, wise Ganesh waved away troubles with his long trunk.

How strange, Neetu thought, as she lay there

in her Indian bed, even in the middle of the night, there is no silence. The air seemed to be throbbing with muffled drums and tinkling bells. Somewhere out there a dog was barking and she wondered why; somewhere out there a man was singing, soft and low, and voices mumbled in prayer. Up in the highest branches of a neem tree, a restless bird squawked sleepily, and Neetu wondered whether birds dream too.

'Neetu!' called Sanjay in a sad, small voice. 'I want to go home.'

'Why, Sanjay?'

'I don't like India. I don't like the smell and it's too noisy.'

Before she could say anything, they heard another sound. It was very close. Neetu sat up, and saw a gleam of light coming from beyond the veranda. She heard the squeal of the pump and the whoosh of water. She slid out of bed and fumbled for her slippers. Sanjay was already sitting, his eyes shining across the room like two moons.

'Where are you going?' he whispered.

'Just to see,' answered Neetu.

'I'm coming too,' muttered Sanjay.

Their feet made no sound on the cool, stone floor as they crossed their room and silently pushed open the door.

Who was that bending over the pump? The moon sparkled silver on the rush of water that flooded out and was tossed over a gleaming body. A cupped hand filled with liquid and a face bent to drink. They heard the water rattle round in the cheeks; another sip and they heard gargling and rinsing and the sound of murmured prayers. Then a jug was lifted, and a cataract of water was poured all over the head. As a towel rubbed the hair and a face finally turned towards them, they saw – it was Grandpa Chatterji.

'What are you doing, Grandpa?' whispered Neetu.

'I'm praying,' answered Grandpa.

'I thought you were washing,' grunted Sanjay.

'Washing is praying,' replied Grandpa with a smile. 'Now I'm going up on the roof to do my exercises, will you come or will you sleep?'

'We'll come,' said Neetu and Sanjay both together.

They climbed the stone steps which curled round from the courtyard and went up on to the flat stone roof with a balustrade all around. They ducked between the criss-cross of washing lines, and passed the television aerial with the paper kite stuck in its prongs, and went round to where they could look across the city all the way to the river, coiling and glinting like a great serpent.

117

First they did stretching and bending, touching
their toes and their heads to their knees and their
knees to their chins and then Grandpa pulled
some dry towels off the washing line and they lay
down on their backs. They lifted each leg and
rotated each ankle, pointed their toes up to the
stars and bent their knees to touch their noses.

'Be a cobra,' said Grandpa, and they rolled on
to their tummies and raised their heads right up.

'Be a bow,' said Grandpa, and they curved their
bodies and stretched their muscles as if you could
shoot arrows from it.

'Be a camel,' said Grandpa, and they knelt with
arms in front and arched their backs like camel's
humps.

'Now I'm going to be a lotus and meditate,' said Grandpa, and they copied him as he sat cross-legged with straight back and hands hung loosely over his knees, and they breathed deeply in and out, in and out . . .

'I feel sleepy,' whispered Sanjay.

'So do I,' nodded Neetu.

They turned to Grandpa, but didn't speak, because he looked as if he had floated away. So they left him. Quietly, they got to their feet and tiptoed across the roof, down the stairs and back to their room.

'Tomorrow, I'm going to play cricket with Rahul,' whispered Sanjay, 'though I wish he'd play football.'

'Tomorrow, I'm going to the kite shop with Radha and we're going to fly kites up on the roof,' said Neetu, 'and we'll see whose kite can fly the highest.'

There was silence. Then Sanjay whispered, 'Neetu, are you awake?'

'No,' came a muffled voice.

'I think I may like India after all.'

'Good,' murmured Neetu and, as if they lay within the petals of a lily, they drifted away into sleep once more.

4

The Cricket Match

'Rahul! Cricket!' the voices called from outside.

'Rahul! Cricket!' repeated Hello, the mynah bird.

Rahul leapt to his feet. He could never say no to a game of cricket.

'Come on, Sanjay, you must play too!'

'I don't play cricket,' shrugged Sanjay. 'I only play football,' and how he wished there was a football around for him to kick.

'Go out and tell them I'm coming in a minute,' cried Rahul, rushing off to his room.

Sanjay wandered out of the gate. Where could they play cricket, anyway? he wondered. Here they were in the middle of the city, and he hadn't noticed any parks or open spaces. He looked up and down the busy road, but couldn't see Rahul's friends.

Then Grandpa Chatterji called out, 'They're in the lane! I'll show you!' The truth was, Grandpa Chatterji loved cricket too, and was always trying to join in. He took Sanjay's hand and led him between the meandering cows and the tinkling bicycles and the hooting, tooting cars and auto-rickshaws and turned the corner into the lane which ran down the side of the house.

'Where's Rahul?' cried the boys. Two or three of them were crouched over some sticks which they were propping up between tin cans.

'He's coming,' answered Sanjay.

When the boys had set their bails, they began to discuss who should bat and bowl first.

'Let me start the batting!' demanded Grandpa,

snatching up a rough piece of wood which had been hacked out to resemble a cricket bat.

The boys grinned. They always let Grandpa Chatterji play for a short while.

'Football's got nothing on cricket,' Grandpa told Sanjay with a wicked smile as he positioned himself in front of the bails. 'Cricket is the best game in the world. I'll make sure you can play it before you go back. Now watch me! Who's bowling?' he called.

A boy called Ashkan tossed an old rubber ball into the air and took up a bowling position while the others rushed to be fielders.

'Hey, Sanjay!' they shouted. 'Stand over there and be an extra till you know how to play.'

Grandpa wriggled his body expectantly and held the bat in front of him, watching the bowler. Ashkan swayed for a moment – to and fro . . . to and fro . . . as if measuring every step. Then he broke into a short run, swung his arm over his head and – pow! The ball hit the bat with a wham and it flew up into the sky.

'Catch, catch, catch!' cried the fielders, rushing towards it with faces upturned. 'Oh!' A groan went up as Tarun, who ran as fast as he could, missed the catch and had to run right out into the road with the cyclists weaving round him and cows blocking his way and the auto-rickshaws tooting and the shopkeepers yelling to tell him where the ball had rolled.

Meanwhile, Grandpa had set off, trying to get in as many runs as he could, and by the time Tarun returned and tossed the ball to Ashkan, Grandpa Chatterji was on his fourth run.

Suddenly Ashkan shouted excitedly. 'Just take a look at Rahul!'

'Wow! He looks like Kapil Dev himself!' the boys exclaimed with awe.

Rahul came striding down the lane – somewhat awkwardly, as he wasn't used to wearing leg-pads, or a helmet or large white padded gloves. In one hand, he brandished a brand-new cricket bat, while in the other was a shiny red-leather cricket ball – the real thing, with white stitching.

The boys clustered round him as if he were a god. With tender hands, they touched his helmet and pads and grasped his gloved hands in theirs. They took it in turns to hold the bat – so shining and oil-bright, and how lovingly they rolled the ball in their hands and tossed it gently into the air, fearing to be the first to drop it and get it all dusty.

'Where did you get this?' they cried with wonderment.

'England!' replied Rahul proudly. 'Sanjay brought it for me from England.'

They all turned and looked at Sanjay, who beamed with pleasure.

'Now I expect you to play like a professional,' said Grandpa, wagging his finger, and he hobbled off to have a rest after all his exertions.

'And look what else I have!' cried Rahul. From under his arm, he extricated three wooden stumps and two bails to go on top. It was the real thing. With whoops of joy, they were snatched from his hands. The tin cans and bits of wood were kicked away into the ditch and the new stumps were carefully propped and wedged with bricks so that they stood upright and the bails balanced on top.

Rahul proudly took his position as batsman and Tarun prepared to bowl the first ball. He set off running, then swung his arm round and up and over. The ball left his hand like a loosed bird, soaring in the air. Rahul kept his eye on it as it hurtled towards him. He swung the bat and – *thwack* – the ball was struck and flew back into the air and the fielders scattered.

All afternoon they played, Rahul allowing each of his friends to use his new kit. Whenever a boy took up the shiny bat and put on the leg-pads and helmet, he felt like Kapil Dev out there on Eden Cricket Ground in Calcutta. He could imagine himself surrounded by thousands of people who had crammed into the ground to see the match; or eagerly peered at by thousands more who couldn't get in, but had climbed up trees and telegraph poles, or begged their way into high windows which overlooked the ground. And when he held the bat, wagging it in front of him, trying to assess at what speed and pace the ball would be bowled to him – it was Imran Khan he imagined facing him, menacingly rubbing every scrap of dust off the ball against his trouser leg.

The bails, balanced on those clean, new stumps, hadn't fallen yet. Then Rahul bowled to Ashkan. Rahul fixed his eye on the stumps. He set off running fast; Ashkan braced himself for a fast spin, but at the last moment, Rahul cunningly changed pace and threw the ball in a wide arc. Ashkan was caught by surprise and the ball spun past him and struck down the stumps and the bails as if they were skittles.

'Yeah!' everyone cheered. Grandpa Chatterji, watching from the veranda, couldn't sit back any longer. He had regained his breath and was ready for more. He longed to try the new bat. He came

leaping out into the lane. 'You don't mind if I just try out the bat, do you?'

'You'd better put on the knee-pads and helmet as well, Grandpa,' laughed Rahul.

Grandpa Chatterji feels like a young boy again. As he stands in front of the wicket, he is back once more in his school's cricket eleven, but he pretends he's playing for Calcutta at Eden Garden. It is an important match. There is a breathless hush. Everyone is depending on him. They need eight more runs to win. Can he pull it off? He taps the ground before him and nervously adjusts the bat in his hands. Then he fixes his eye on the ball. It is not Rahul standing before him ready to bowl, but the great Sunil Gavaskar. A figure is bounding towards him. With what grace his arm goes back and round and over. The red ball comes spinning through the air. But it can't escape his eye. He swings the bat with a rapid swipe and strikes the ball with all his might. The sound of leather on willow echoes all around. A gasp goes up from the boys, but to Grandpa Chatterji, it sounds like the gasp from fifteen thousand people – no – from the whole of India, whose ears are glued to radios, and eyes to television. The nation comes to a standstill and holds its breath.

He sets off running. He'll easily get those runs and his team will win. Strange. The yells of triumph have turned to groans of despair.

'Oh no! Now you've gone and done it, Grandpa!' wailed Rahul.

The red leather ball had sailed far over their upstretched hands; far over the road, honking with traffic; far over the stalls of the astonished shop-keepers; over a far distant wall it went and out of sight.

The boys chased after it. They tried to climb the wall – balancing on shoulders and heaving each other up – but it was too high. Groaning with dejection, they gave up and went home. They all knew whose house it had fallen into. Dr

Ranjit Bose was the grumpiest man in Calcutta. He was always chasing off the boys. He would never give them back the ball.

Rahul didn't say a word, but went silently to his room. Sanjay went over to sit with Great Grandma and chat to Hello. Grandpa Chatterji took himself off to the veranda and sat cross-legged on his mat. He closed his eyes and breathed deeply. Into his brain, came the image of a shiny, round red-leather cricket ball with white stitching.

At tea-time, Rahul was still too upset to speak and he wouldn't sit next to his grandfather.

'Don't be too upset, Rahul,' Neetu tried to comfort him. 'We'll send you another ball from England.'

'How can you?' grunted Rahul dejectedly.

129

'You can't just post a cricket ball.'

'Someone may find it and return it to you,' suggested Grandpa gently. 'You never know.'

'I know,' declared Rahul, scornfully. 'Who would return such a ball if they found it? Especially not Dr Bose.'

'We'll see,' murmured Grandpa Chatterji.

When Grandma saw all those long faces, she brought out her cakes – even though they were really meant for Sunday tea. She knew a tragedy had befallen them.

Suddenly, a shadow, no thicker than a toothpick, fell across the dorrway.

'*Korn?*' demanded Hello in Great Grandma's voice.

There stood a thin, gangly, bony boy in grey school shorts and white shirt, looking very awkward and shy.

'Come in, come in, come in!' urged Aunty Meena kindly.

The boy slipped off his sandals and stepped inside.

'Can we help you?' asked Grandpa, as the boy seemed very tongue-tied.

'My grandfather . . . Dr Bose . . .'

There was an intake of breath from everyone.

'My grandfather asks if any of you lost a

cricket ball this morning?' I asked round the district and the shopkeepers sent me here.'

'I lost a cricket ball!' shouted Rahul excitedly. 'A brand-new, shiny, red-leather cricket ball, all the way from England.'

'My grandfather would like you to call and collect it,' the boy stammered. 'Can you come with me, now?'

Rahul looked at his grandfather with alarm. What, go to Dr Bose's house and risk getting his ears boxed? 'Can't you go, Grandpa?' he begged.

'Go, Rahul. Go with the boy,' said Grandpa reassuringly. 'You see. It will be all right. I know it will.'

So Rahul put on his shoes and went with the boy to the house of Dr Bose.

It was a great, crumbling, old-style house, with lots of shuttered windows and balconies overflowing with flowerpots and creepers. He followed the boy up long, stone veranda steps, through shadowed arches and into a darkened living room.

'*Korn?*' asked a gruff old man's voice from within the depths of a deep armchair.

'It's me, Grandfather, Amu. I've found the owner of the cricket ball.'

'Let me see him then,' and a thin, gnarled hand waved them before him.

Rahul edged round the chair to face Dr Bose, but stood at a safe distance, out of reach.

'Come closer, boy, stand where I ccan see you properly,' the old man croaked impatiently.

Rahul came forward and stood directly in front. He had never really looked at Dr Bose before. Now he saw an aged face, creased with pain, but with eagle-sharp eyes which peered up at him from behind steel-rimmed spectacles.

'Who hit the ball into my garden? Was it you?'

'No, sir, not exactly . . .' stammered Rahul.

'Not exactly? What is this – not exactly? Did you or didn't you?'

'I bowled the ball, sir, but my grandfather batted it. He got a bit carried away because it is a

real cricket ball from England,' explained Rahul apologetically.

'Is this the ball?' The old man held up a red-leather cricket ball.

'Yes, sir, that's mine!' Rahul stared longingly at the ball. He wanted to grab it and run away from this sad, gloomy house.

'I'll give you back your ball but only in exchange for a favour,' said the old man.

Rahul waited respectfully, wondering what possible favour he could do for Dr Bose.

'This is my grandson, Amar. Come here, Amu, stand where I can see you!' he commanded.

The bony boy shuffled round and stood next to Rahul. Rahul glanced at him and realised that they were both about the same age.

'Amar is down from boarding school to stay

with me for the holidays. It's lonely for him, stuck with a decrepit old man like me. So, in exchange for returning your cricket ball, will you allow Amar to play cricket with you?'

'Of course, sir, of course!' cried Rahul with relief. 'Come any time you like! We're always playing,' he told the boy.

Amu's face broke into a wide-open smile.

As Amu was leading Rahul away, Dr Bose suddenly called out, 'By the way, that grandfather of yours is quite a cricketer. He must have given that ball a terrific swipe for it to reach my garden. Send him my congratulations, will you?'

'Oh yes, sir! Indeed, sir!' laughed Rahul.

The next day the boys were out again in the lane. They propped up the stumps and bails with the bricks and picked the fielders and the batsmen. Rahul stood at the wicket in all his gear. He held the bat expectantly, becoming Kapil Dev again in his mind's eye. Amar faced him as the bowler. Rahul's friends felt a bit nervous about having Dr Bose's grandson to play — especially as he didn't look as if he could swat a fly, let alone play cricket. He held the ball in his hand, then rubbed it against his shorts. Nervously, he clenched and unclenched his knobbly knees, then with a nod at

Rahul, he began his run. His charge was swift and surprising. His arm whirled round and he let loose a deceptive fast ball. It flew through the air and skidded on the loose dust, homing in on the stumps. Rahul instinctively got down to it and lifted the ball with the meat of the bat. THWACK. The ball seemed to balloon out. It soared out over the mid-on and over all the fielders running with their arms outstretched. It began to fall exactly over Sanjay, who had been standing in again at extra cover.

'Catch it, catch it, catch it!' the voices shrieked.

For an instant, Sanjay was bewildered. Then he heard Grandpa Chatterji's voice shouting, 'Sanjay! Look at the ball! Put up your arms, open your hands!'

Sanjay looked up and saw the ball plummeting down on him. He held up his arms and opened his hands. Plop! The ball dropped straight into his fingers. Its force threw him to the ground, but he didn't let go. He rolled over with the ball clutched to his chest, while everyone rushed around him.

'Well done, Sanjay!' they yelled, and lifted him up on to their shoulders as if he were a hero.

On the other side of the street, two old men watched the game from a tea shop.

'They're not too bad, those grandsons of ours,

eh?' Dr Bose's eyes twinkled as he poured Grandpa Chatterji another cup of tea.

That night, before dropping off to sleep, Sanjay asked his dad, 'Do you think I could have a cricket kit for my next birthday?'

Dad grinned with pleasure. 'I'll speak to Mum about it.'

5

Grandma's Cakes

All around the house came the sound of children's voices. They were playing hide-and-seek. Everyone joined in. They raced in and out of the rooms, across the courtyard, up the stone steps on to the roof, down again, on to the veranda and out into the garden. Their voices rose as they counted, yelled, giggled, snuffled and shuffled into their hiding places, shushing each other up and stifling their laughter. Then there would be a brief silence while the seeker went seeking.

Sassu was hiding her eyes and counting. Neetu looked unsure of where to hide, but Radha grabbed her arm and said, 'Come with me! I'll show you a good place.' Everyone scuttled off in all directions.

A wonderful warm smell was wafting through

the house. It followed the children wherever they went. There was no hiding place where the delicious sweet aroma didn't reach and make them smack their lips.

'What's that nice smell?' whispered Neetu, as she crouched next to Radha in their hiding place behind the wardrobe.

'Is today Friday?' asked Radha. 'Then it's Grandma's baking day.'

They heard Sassu shout, 'Coming!' and saw her rush past. They heard her stop at the kitchen to see if anyone was hiding there, and then carry on up to the roof.

Radha and Neetu crept out. 'Sassu's checked the kitchen and she won't come back. Let's see if

Grandma needs help with her cakes.'

Grandma Chatterji stood there with a large mixing bowl in her arms, stirring and stirring – flour, butter, eggs, milk, sugar, nuts and raisins. Her oven was already hot and glowing with one batch of cakes. Now she began to spoon out her mixture on to a cupped tray for another batch.

Radha and Neetu appeared in the doorway. 'Can we help with the cakes?' asked Radha coming up to the mixing bowl and dipping in a finger.

'*Arreh!* Don't go poking your fingers in my bowl!' snapped Grandma sternly. Aren't you meant to be hiding?'

Neetu felt a little afraid of Grandma because she could look so fierce. She seemed to make the rules in the house and everyone obeyed her. Neetu shyly tugged Radha's hand and whispered, 'We'd better go back to our hiding place before Sassu finds us.'

But Radha wasn't afraid. She circled Grandma, scooping up bits of cake mixture with her little finger.

'Stop it, Radha!' Grandma ordered and smacked her granddaughter's hand. 'She's such a naughty girl – don't you think so, Neetu? She's as bad as the sparrows.

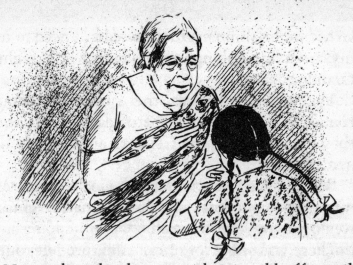

Neetu thought they were being told off, until she saw Grandma's light brown eyes – which could be as hard as walnuts – sparkling with friendliness. Grandma finished spooning out the mixture on to the tray, and then, to their joy, offered them the bowl and spoon to lick.

Suddenly, a cluster of sparrows hurtled in through the fretwork which criss-crossed the open kitchen window. Chirruping excitedly in hectic play, they darted and dived among the kitchen shelves.

'Arreh, these sparrows! They're such a nuisance. They do potty potty all over the place! Grandpa wants to put a wire mesh over the windows, but I won't let him. A wire mesh may stop the sparrows, but it would make my kitchen

141

so hot in the summer, that I wouldn't need to use my oven for baking. So, what to do?' sighed Grandma.

The girls ducked as the sparrows zoomed round, weaving in and out of each other, then they dived through the fretwork and out into the garden again.

'Well, I suppose they are all God's creatures,' murmured Grandma, 'and have as many rights as we do. So, we'll let them be.'

There was still a lot of cake mixture left round the sides of the bowl when they heard footsteps coming.

'Quick! Sassu's coming!' exclaimed Radha. 'We'd better hide,' and she dragged Neetu away back to their hiding place behind the wardrobe.

But it wasn't Sassu. It was Sanjay who appeared in the doorway, his mouth watering with the smell of the baking cakes.

'Hello, Sanjay!' said Grandma. 'Aren't you meant to be hiding?'

'I don't know a good place,' complained Sanjay, his eyes on the bowl and spoon which were still thick with cake mixture. 'Hmmm!' He slid a finger round the inside of the mixing bowl. 'Are these cakes for us?' he asked, fervently sucking his finger.

'Yes,' said Grandma, taking one batch out of the oven and putting in another.

Sanjay's hand stretched out hopefully, but Grandma flicked it away with a frown. 'No, Sanjay. These are for tea on Sunday,' and she looked so severe, that Sanjay didn't dare beg to let him have just one! 'But here, child,' she said with a sudden glinting smile, 'you can lick the spoon if you like.'

Sanjay eagerly snatched the spoon she offered and began to lick it all over: up the stem, round the neck, and he was just getting to the really thick bit on the head, when suddenly Sassu appeared and grabbed him. 'I've caught Sanjay! Now it's his turn to hide his eyes.'

'That's not fair,' moaned Sanjay. 'I wasn't even hiding!'

'Well, you should have been!' cried Sassu unmercifully.

The other children appeared flushed and laughing. They made Sanjay stand by a veranda pillar and hide his eyes. 'No peeping,' Rahul warned him. 'And be sure to count to a hundred!'

'Sanjay can't count to a hundred!' scoffed Neetu.

'Oh yes, I can!' retorted Sanjay and began chanting loudly: one . . . two . . . three . . .

The children scattered. Sanjay did get stuck around fifteen, so he went back to the beginning and started again, getting quieter and quieter till be was murmuring softly and waiting a long enough time so that it would seem as though he had counted to a hundred. Then he yelled, 'COMING!'

'COMING!' echoed Hello from out in the courtyard, and burst out cackling.

Sanjay wandered about from room to room; he looked under beds, behind chairs and sofas; he tugged at curtains in case someone was coiled up inside them and climbed up on to the roof to search among the washing lines flapping with clothes. But his heart wasn't really in it. He couldn't stop thinking about Grandma's cakes. He went back to the kitchen, but the bowl and spoon had been cleared away. Grandma had finished her baking and gone to wash her hair under the courtyard tap. He lingered, held by the rich warm smell, and wondered where Grandma had stored her cakes. He looked around, pretending he was hunting for the others. Perhaps someone was hiding under the table or in the cupboard.

Suddenly, he saw a movement behind a far curtain. He dashed over and flung it aside.

'Caught you!' he shouted triumphantly.

'Sssh!' It was Grandpa Chatterji, looking extremely guilty, with a cake clutched in his fingers. Behind the curtain was a small pantry, and standing in a corner was a metal chest. 'I was just checking to see if Grandma's cakes were up to her usual standard,' he exclaimed with a smile like a wicked robber. 'Aren't you meant to be looking for everyone! Go on! Be off with you! There's no one hiding here.' Grandpa Chatterji drew aside the curtain and bustled Sanjay out of the kitchen. 'Now I must get along to the post office.' And Grandpa Chatterji hurried away.

Sanjay couldn't help himself; he went back into the kitchen. A sparrow flew in through the window and darted behind the curtain into the

pantry. Sanjay followed. The sparrow chirruped on the ledge above the tin chest and cocked his head sideways, looking with an eager eye. A rich warm sugary smell hung in the air. Sanjay lifted the lid. There were the newly baked cakes, stored like gold. There were several layers all lined up on their trays, with clean white napkins in between.

'I wonder if Grandma's cakes are up to standard?' said Sanjay to himself. He bent down and sniffed and before he knew it, he had stuffed one cake into his mouth and swallowed it.

'That one seems to be up to standard,' he murmured, brushing away the crumbs from his chin. The sparrow flew down quickly to peck as a large black ant peered out of a crack in the wall. 'I wonder if they are all as good as that.'

The sparrow spun in the air expectantly. Sanjay wriggled a hand down the side. There were many layers of cakes. Perhaps he should check one cake from each layer. He lifted out another.

Puzzled voices were ringing round the house. 'Sanjay! Come and find me!' Gradually, it began to dawn on those who were hiding, that Sanjay wasn't looking for them. They came out feeling annoyed. 'Sanjay! Where are you?' shouted Rahul. 'If you don't play properly, we won't let you join in our games!'

But there was no sign of Sanjay. Now everyone was looking for him. Inside and outside and up on the roof and all round the garden. They even looked in the lane outside the house, calling and calling his name.

The grown-ups were consulted. 'Have you seen Sanjay?' they asked Grandma Chatterji, who was drying her hair in the sun.

'Have you seen Sanjay?' they asked Aunty Meena who was shelling peas on the veranda.

'Have you seen Sanjay?' they whispered to Great Grandma Chatterji. But she was dozing, and Hello called out, 'Sanjay! Naughty boy, naughty boy!'

Grandpa Chatterji came walking back from the post office. 'We've lost Sanjay. Is he with you?' they asked.

'No . . .' Grandpa looked thoughtful.

Suddenly Grandma shouted, '*Arreh!* Look at all those ants coming from my kitchen!'

A long, long trail of large, shining black ants came out of the kitchen, across the veranda, down the steps and trooped out into the garden.

'Look, look, look! They're carrying

something,' exclaimed Aunty Meena.

Everyone bent down to look. 'Cake crumbs!' cried Grandma. 'Has someone been eating my cakes?'

The sight of all those ants made Neetu's skin prickle, but she couldn't help being fascinated by the busy, determined creatures, moving to and fro in a constantly flowing line, as they shunted cake crumbs from one to another.

'I hope they haven't got at Grandma's cakes,' muttered Radha.

Grandma Chatterji looked accusingly at Grandpa Chatterji. 'Have you been at my cakes again?' she demanded sternly. She knew what a weakness Grandpa had for her cakes.

Before Grandpa could reply, they all heard a faint whimpering. They hurried into the kitchen. The train of ants crossed the floor and disappeared behind the curtain. Radha ran over and flung the curtain aside and Neetu gave a shriek of horror. There stood Sanjay on top of the tin chest with a cake in each hand. Crumbs and tears dripped from his cheeks. He was surrounded by a vast sea of black ants.

'Silly India, silly India,' he whimpered.

Grandpa Chatterji plunged through the swarming creatures and held open his arms.

Sanjay leapt into them gratefully, whispering, 'I'm sorry, I'm sorry, I'm sorry!'

'Oh, Sanjay!' cried Neetu. 'You naughty boy. You've been stealing Grandma's cakes.'

'Don't blame Sanjay,' Grandma said sternly. 'He learned it from someone who should have known better!' and she wagged her finger at Grandpa Chatterji. 'No cakes for you this week!' she said.

Grandpa Chatterji bowed his head. 'Sorry!'

'Sorree,' squawked Hello, solemnly.

The children all burst out laughing. 'Sanjay had such a good hiding place, no one would have found him if it hadn't been for the ants!' they shouted, then like a flock of sparrows, rushed off again to play.

Grandpa beckoned Sanjay and whispered in his ear, 'In India, food is very precious. Nothing goes to waste. If you drop one crumb, there is always a pig, a dog, a monkey, a cockroach, a sparrow or an ant to come and eat it up. So next time, be sure not to drop a single crumb.'

Sanjay nodded, then whispered back, 'Grandpa, can you show me another good hiding place?'

The River

'Before you go home to England, you must bathe in the river. Today, we are going to take Great Grandma Chatterji for her bathe, so you can go too,' said Grandpa Chatterji.

Neetu and Sanjay were amazed. Why, Great Grandma even had to be helped to the pump in the courtyard. How could she want to go to the river to bathe?

But no one seemed surprised.

Great Grandma liked to go in a horse-drawn carriage, so that afternoon Uncle Ashok set off to find one. Soon he returned and came trit-trotting up to the gates in a carriage like the ones Neetu and Sanjay had seen in films or pictures of Victorian England – and it was called a victoria. It was pulled by two smart horses – one brown, one white, with shiny leather and brass-embossed harness and each with a red feathered plume between its ears. The driver sat on a high seat at the front, the reins dangling between the fingers of one hand and a long, long whip in the other, with which to flick the horses into action.

First, Aunty Meena and Uncle Ashok carefully helped Great Grandma to the carriage and settled her in; then Grandpa held open the carriage door like a footman, and Neetu and Sanjay climbed inside and sank back into the red-leather seats.

So that they had plenty of room, Uncle Ashok said he and Aunty Meena would follow them on his motor-scooter.

The horses set off clip-clopping, their hooves echoing down the broad Calcutta streets. Neetu and Sanjay studied the old old lady who sat before them all wrapped up in her shawl. 'Is Great Grandma really going to bathe in the river?' they asked in puzzled voices.

'Oh, yes,' said Grandpa Chatterji. 'The river has become the most important place in her life.'

They stared out of the carriage windows as the horses trotted out into the road and joined a human river – a river of people who swept through that huge city, pulling things, pushing things, carrying things, – on their backs and on their heads; there were those who were riding on

bicycles, mopeds, in rickshaws or in trams and buses; it was a torrent of living creatures among which wandered dogs and pigs and horses and cows, where birds swooped and flapped and squawked and soared over the rooftops with the hundreds of fluttering paper kites.

Then Grandpa cried out, 'Look!'

They saw the huge, curving girders of a bridge which stretched over a wide expanse of shining water. It looked as though it had been built to carry the weight of the whole of mankind.

When they had crossed to the other side, they made their way along the river until they came to a place where many people had gathered.

The sunlight danced on the water, sparkling and shimmering. All sorts of boats and crafts floated like dreams through the liquid haze. Men, women and children stood at the water's edge, their garments fluttering. They bent and scooped water into their hands and rubbed their arms and faces, then they walked further into the river and finally dipped themselves under completely.

'This is where Great Grandma likes to bathe,' said Grandpa Chatterji, as the horses pulled up.

Neetu and Sanjay watched wonderingly, as Uncle Ashok and Aunty Meena led Great Grandma between them, down to the water's

edge. There, she removed her shawl and her slippers, put everything in a neat pile, and let out her hair. Uncle Ashok and Aunty Meena did the same then, each with an arm round Great Grandma to support her, they all entered the water and waded out until they stood waist-deep.

Garlands of marigolds and hollowed-out coconut shells floated around them as they cupped their hands and scooped water over their heads and drank and chanted prayers.

'But why do they need to go into the river to pray?' asked Neetu.

So Grandpa Chatterji told them.

'Once, many thousands of years ago, when the world was still being created, this river only flowed in heaven, high up beyond the highest peaks of the Himalayan mountains. The river was really the goddess Ganga, and her waters were so holy, that anyone who bathed in them would be cleansed of their sins and gain everlasting life.

There was a king living on earth – at a time when the world had only just been created and things were very new. This king had two wives, but no children, so he prayed devotedly to God and, at last, he was rewarded with the birth of many sons. The king was so happy that he looked for the finest horse in the land to sacrifice to God in gratitude.

At last he found the strongest, most beautiful, pure white horse and captured it, not realising that it belonged to Lord Indra. Before the horse could be sacrificed, Indra stole it back again. The king and his sons searched high and low for the horse, for they couldn't think of anything else that was good enough to offer to God. His sons even dug their way through to the centre of the earth looking for this horse. They dug so deep, that the goddess of the earth cried out in pain and her husband, Lord Vishnu, sent a terrible fire which burned the king's sons to death.

The king was grief-stricken. He hadn't meant
to offend anybody and he begged God to bring his
sons back to life. God told him, 'Your sons will
come back to life when the River Ganga flows to
earth.'

So now the king began years and years of
praying and penance. At last, God was moved and
allowed the goddess Ganga to flow to earth.

The river eagerly gathered herself together in a
mighty torrent ready to plunge to earth, when
Lord Shiva, the blue-throated one, the destroyer
of evil, realised that the whole world would be
destroyed by the river's force. As the heavens

opened, he stood underneath and the great cataract thundered down on his head.

The great river was trapped in Shiva's tangled hair, and for a while, wandered over his head looking for ways to escape. Finally, she found seven partings in his hair and, breaking herself up, she was at last released from Shiva's head and flowed to earth, broken up into seven rivers. The pure mountain waters of the River Ganga tumbled down and with it came fish and turtles and porpoises and frogs and crocodiles and spray, which scattered like egrets. It was marvellous. Even the gods and angels and heavenly warriors, glistening with jewels, were amazed.

The rivers broke into streams and brooks and waterfalls and pools, and tumbled merrily down on to the arid plains, soaking deep into the earth. Trickles of it came to the ashes of the king's sons. As the waters mingled with their ashes, their souls came to life and ascended into heaven to live in happiness for ever.'

'So you see,' explained Grandpa Chatterji, 'the river Hooghly is one of those rivers and that is why people come to bathe here. They hope that when they die, their ashes will be put into the river so that their souls will go up to heaven.'

The children watched as Uncle Ashok and Aunty Meena helped Great Grandma to submerge herself completely in the water.

'Here, take these towels to them and a set of dry clothes to change into – and you can bathe too if you wish,' smiled Grandpa Chatterji.

'We didn't bring a change of clothes,' said Neetu in a disappointed voice.

'Oh, never mind. Go and bathe. Just take your shoes off,' said Grandpa.

'Can we really go in with all our clothes on?' cried Neetu and Sanjay with delight.

'The sun is so hot that if you run up and down for half an hour, you'll soon dry,' said Grandpa.

Neetu and Sanjay ran excitedly down to the water, but then both stopped before rushing in. They remembered Grandpa's story. This was no ordinary water. This river was holy. Sanjay took Neetu's hand, and feeling suddenly solemn, they stepped into the silky water.

'Look!' whispered Neetu pointing towards mid-river.

A great turtle seemed to swim specially close, so that they could see his shiny shell-back, his delicate but powerful arms and feet, and his smooth, gentle head, then he dived and disappeared from view.

Grandpa Chatterji watched his grandchildren with great contentment. He was glad that they had bathed in the waters of the Ganga before going back home to England.